CLASSICS ILLUSTRATED GRAPHIC NOVELS AVAILABLE FROM PAPERCUTZ

CLASSICS ILLUSTRATED DELUXE:

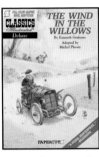

#5 "Treasure Island"

#4 "The Adventures of Tom Sawyer"

#3 "Frankenstein"

#1 "The Wind In The Willows"

#2 "Tales From The Brothers Grimm"

CLASSICS ILLUSTRATED:

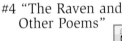

#5 "Hamlet"

#4 "The Raven and Other Poems"

#1 "Great Expectations"

#2 "The Invisible Man"

#3 "Through the Looking-Glass"

Coming June '10
#10 "Cyrano de Bergerac"

Coming April '10
#9 "The Jungle"

#6 "The Scarlet Letter"

#7 "Dr. Jekyll & Mr. Hyde"

#8 "The Count of Monte Cristo"

Classics Illustrated Deluxe are available for $13.95 each in paperback and $17.95 in hardcover.
Classics Illustrated are available only in hardcover for $9.95 each, except #8, 9, 10, $9.99.
Please add $4.00 for postage and handling for the first book, add $1.00 for each additional book.
MC, Visa, Amex accepted or make check payable to NBM Publishing.
Send to: Papercutz, 40 Exchange Place, Suite 1308, New York, NY 10005 • 1-800-866-1223

WWW.PAPERCUTZ.COM

Deluxe

#5

TREASURE ISLAND

BY ROBERT LOUIS STEVENSON
ADAPTED BY DAVID CHAUVEL, FRED SIMON, AND JEAN-LUC SIMON

New York

Thanks to Christophe Araldi for his help with the book covers. The back cover design was inspired by a painting by the illustrator Howard Pyle.
The authors

For Ivan, my very own pirate.
Papa
For Catherine.
F.S.

Treasure Island
By Robert Louis Stevenson
Adapted by David Chauvel, Fred Simon, and Jean-Luc Simon

Translation by Joe Johnson
Lettering by Ortho
John Haufe and William B. Jones Jr. — Classics Illustrated Historians
Michael Petranek — Editorial Assistant
Jim Salicrup
Editor-in-Chief

ISBN: 978-1-59707-184-0 paperback edition
ISBN: 978-1-59707-185-7 hardcover edition

Printed in China.
November 2009 by Regent Printing
6/F Hang Tung Resource Centre No. 18
A Kung Ngam Village Road
Shau Kei Wan, Hong Kong

Distributed by Macmillan.

10 9 8 7 6 5 4 3 2 1

I REMEMBER HIM AS IF IT WERE YESTERDAY, AS HE CAME PLODDING TO THE INN DOOR, HIS SEA CHEST FOLLOWING BEHIND HIM.

HE WAS A TALL, STRONG MAN; AND THE SABER CUT ACROSS ONE CHEEK, A DIRTY, LIVID WHITE.

FIFTEEN MEN ON THE DEAD MAN'S CHEST YO-HO-HO, AND A BOTTLE OF RUM!

HE SANG IN A HIGH, OLD, TOTTERING VOICE THAT SEEMED TO HAVE BEEN TUNED AND BROKEN AT THE CAPSTAN BARS.

TOC
TOC

COME IN!

A GLASS OF RUM!

THERE.

THIS IS A HANDY COVE AND A PLEASANT, SITTYATED GROGSHOP. MUCH COMPANY, MATE?

ALAS, NO, NOT ENOUGH.

ALL THE BETTER!

I'LL STAY HERE A BIT. I'M A PLAIN MAN; RUM AND BACON AND EGGS IS WHAT I WANT, AND THAT HEAD UP THERE FOR TO WATCH SHIPS OFF.

OH, I SEE WHAT YOU'RE AT THERE.

CLINK CLINK CLINK

YOU CAN TELL ME WHEN I'VE WORKED THROUGH THAT.

AND THAT WAS ALL WE COULD LEARN OF OUR GUEST.

HE WAS A VERY SILENT MAN BY CUSTOM.

ALL DAY HE HUNG ROUND THE COVE OR UPON THE CLIFFS, WITH A BRASS TELESCOPE IN HAND.

ALL EVENING HE SAT IN A CORNER OF THE PARLOR NEXT THE FIRE, AND DRANK RUM AND WATER VERY STRONG.

EVERY DAY, WHEN HE CAME BACK FROM HIS STROLL, HE WOULD ASK IF ANY SEAFARING MEN HAD GONE ALONG BY THE ROAD.

HE HAD TAKEN ME ASIDE ONE DAY AND PROMISED ME...

A SILVER FOUR-PENNY ON THE FIRST OF EVERY MONTH IF YOU'LL KEEP YOUR WEATHER EYE OPEN FOR A SEAFARING MAN WITH ONE LEG.

DO YOU UNDERSTAND, BOY? A SEAFARING MAN WITH ONE LEG!

THERE WERE NIGHTS WHEN HE TOOK A DEAL MORE RUM AND WATER THAN HIS HEAD COULD CARRY; AND THEN HE WOULD SOMETIMES SIT AND SING HIS WICKED, OLD, WILD SEA SONGS, MINDING NOBODY.

HIS STORIES WERE WHAT FRIGHTENED PEOPLE WORST OF ALL.

DREADFUL STORIES THEY WERE: ABOUT HANGINGS, TORTURE, AND ATTACKS ON SPANISH ENCLAVES IN THE AMERICAS.

HE KEPT ON STAYING WEEK AFTER WEEK, AND AT LAST MONTH AFTER MONTH, SO THAT ALL THE MONEY HAD BEEN LONG EXHAUSTED.

STILL MY FATHER NEVER PLUCKED UP THE HEART TO INSIST ON HAVING MORE.

HE WAS ONLY ONCE CROSSED, AND THAT WAS TOWARD THE END, WHEN MY POOR FATHER WAS FAR GONE IN A DECLINE THAT TOOK HIM OFF.

DR. LIVESEY CAME LATE ONE AFTERNOON TO SEE THE PATIENT.

MY MOTHER HAD SERVED HIM A LIGHT SUPPER, AND HE WENT INTO THE PARLOR TO SMOKE A PIPE UNTIL HIS HORSE SHOULD COME DOWN FROM THE HAMLET, FOR WE HAD NO STABLING AT THE OLD "BENBOW."

FIFTEEN MEN ON THE DEAD MAN'S CHEST ♪ YO-HO-HO, ♪ AND A BOTTLE OF RUM!

DRINK AND THE DEVIL HAD DONE FOR THE REST ♪ YO-HO-HO ♪ AND A BOTTLE OF RUM!

DR. LIVESEY LOOKED UP FOR A MOMENT QUITE ANGRILY BEFORE HE WENT ON WITH HIS TALK TO OLD TAYLOR, THE GARDENER.

SILENCE, THERE, BETWEEN DECKS!!

WERE YOU ADDRESSING ME, SIR?

BY THE DEVIL, OF COURSE IT'S YOU!!

I HAVE ONLY ONE THING TO SAY TO YOU, SIR...

...THAT IF YOU KEEP ON DRINKING RUM, THE WORLD WILL SOON BE QUIT OF A VERY DIRTY SCOUNDREL.

IF YOU DO NOT PUT THAT SABER AWAY THIS INSTANT, I PROMISE, UPON MY HONOR, YOU SHALL HANG AT THE NEXT ASSIZES.

I'M NOT A DOCTOR ONLY, I'M A MAGISTRATE.

AND IF I CATCH A BREATH OF COMPLAINT AGAINST YOU, IF IT'S ONLY FOR A PIECE OF INCIVILITY LIKE TONIGHT'S, I'LL TAKE EFFECTUAL MEANS TO HAVE YOU HUNTED DOWN AND ROUTED OUT OF THIS.

LET THAT SUFFICE.

IT WAS NOT VERY LONG AFTER THIS THAT THERE OCCURRED THE FIRST OF THE MYSTERIOUS EVENTS THAT RID US AT LAST OF THE CAPTAIN, THOUGH NOT, AS YOU WILL SEE, OF HIS AFFAIRS.

IT WAS A BITTER COLD WINTER, AND IT WAS PLAIN FROM THE FIRST THAT MY POOR FATHER WAS LITTLE LIKELY TO SEE THE SPRING.

THE CAPTAIN HAD RISEN EARLIER THAN USUAL AND SET DOWN THE BEACH, HIS BRASS TELESCOPE UNDER HIS ARM, HIS HAT TILTED BACK UPON HIS HEAD.

I WAS LAYING THE BREAKFAST TABLE WHEN THE PARLOR DOOR OPENED AND A MAN STEPPED IN.

THOUGH HE WORE A CUTLASS, HE DID NOT LOOK MUCH LIKE A FIGHTER. HE WAS NOT SAILORLY, AND YET HE HAD A SMACK OF THE SEA ABOUT HIM, TOO.

HOW CAN I BE OF SERVICE, SIR?

I'LL HAVE SOME RUM!

IS THIS HERE TABLE FOR MY MATE BILL?

HE HAS A CUT ON ONE CHEEK AND A MIGHTY PLEASANT WAY WITH HIM, PARTICULARLY IN DRINK.

I DON'T KNOW YOUR MATE BILL.

IS HE HERE IN THE HOUSE?

NO, HE WENT TO TAKE A WALK ON THE CLIFF.

THIS TABLE IS FOR A PERSON WHO'S STAYING IN OUR HOUSE, WHOM WE CALL THE CAPTAIN.

AH, THIS'LL BE AS GOOD AS DRINK TO MY MATE BILL.

THE STRANGER KEPT HANGING ABOUT JUST INSIDE THE INN DOOR, PEERING ROUND THE CORNER LIKE A CAT WAITING FOR A MOUSE.

THERE'S MY MATE BILL!!

LET'S GET BEHIND THE DOOR, AND WE'LL GIVE BILL A LITTLE SURPRISE, BLESS HIS 'ART, I SAY AGAIN.

BILL.

COME, BILL, YOU KNOW ME, YOU KNOW AN OLD SHIPMATE, BILL, SURELY.

BLACK DOG!

AND WHO ELSE? BLACK DOG AS EVER WAS, COME FOR TO SEE HIS OLD SHIPMATE BILLY, AT THE ADMIRAL BENBOW INN.

NOW, LOOK HERE, YOU'VE RUN ME DOWN; HERE I AM; WELL, THEN, SPEAK UP: WHAT IS IT?

THAT'S YOU, BILL!

GO DO YOUR SWEEPING, BOY, AND NONE OF YOUR KEYHOLES FOR ME, SONNY!

YOU'RE IN THE RIGHT OF IT, BILLY. I'LL HAVE A GLASS OF RUM FROM THIS DEAR CHILD HERE, AS I'VE TOOK SUCH A LIKING, TOO, AND WE'LL SIT DOWN, IF YOU PLEASE, AND TALK SQUARE, LIKE OLD SHIPMATES.

FOR A LONG TIME, THOUGH I CERTAINLY DID MY BEST TO LISTEN, I COULD HEAR NOTHING BUT A LOW GABBLING.

NO, NO, NO, NO; AND AN END OF IT!

IF IT COMES TO SWINGING, SWING ALL, SAY I.

BY ALL THE DEVILS! YOU ASKED FOR IT!

AAAH!

AT LAST THE VOICES BEGAN TO GROW HIGHER.

TCHOK

I MUST GET AWAY FROM HERE.

JIM, RUM! RUM! RUM!

BAM

AT THE SAME INSTANT MY MOTHER, ALARMED BY THE CRIES AND THE FIGHTING, CAME RUNNING DOWNSTAIRS TO HELP ME.

DEARY ME!

WHAT A DISGRACE UPON THE HOUSE! AND YOUR POOR FATHER SICK!

IT WAS A HAPPY RELIEF FOR US WHEN THE DOOR OPENED AND DR. LIVESEY CAME IN, ON HIS VISIT TO MY FATHER.

OH, DOCTOR, WHAT SHALL WE DO?

WHERE IS HE WOUNDED?

WOUNDED?

THE MAN HAS HAD A STROKE, AS I WARNED HIM. NOW, MRS. HAWKINS, JUST RUN UPSTAIRS TO YOUR HUSBAND AND TELL HIM, IF POSSIBLE, NOTHING ABOUT IT.

WHERE'S BLACK DOG?

THERE IS NO BLACK DOG HERE, EXCEPT WHAT YOU HAVE ON YOUR OWN BACK. YOU HAVE BEEN DRINKING RUM; YOU HAVE HAD A STROKE, PRECISELY AS I TOLD YOU.

ONE GLASS OF RUM WON'T KILL YOU, BUT IF YOU TAKE ONE YOU'LL TAKE ANOTHER AND ANOTHER, AND I STAKE MY WIG IF YOU DON'T BREAK OFF SHORT YOU'LL DIE.

BETWEEN US, WITH MUCH TROUBLE, WE MANAGED TO HOIST HIM UPSTAIRS AND LAID HIM ON HIS BED.

HE SHOULD LIE FOR A WEEK WHERE HE IS--THAT IS THE BEST THING FOR HIM AND YOU; BUT ANOTHER STROKE WOULD SETTLE HIM.

ABOUT NOON I STOPPED AT THE CAPTAIN'S DOOR WITH SOME COOLING DRINKS AND MEDICINES.

HE WAS LYING VERY MUCH AS WE HAD LEFT HIM AND HE SEEMED BOTH WEAK AND EXCITED.

JIM, YOU KNOW I'VE BEEN ALWAYS GOOD TO YOU.

AND NOW YOU SEE, MATE, I'M PRETTY LOW AND DESERTED BY ALL; AND, JIM, YOU'LL BRING ME ONE NOGGIN OF RUM, NOW, WON'T YOU, MATEY?

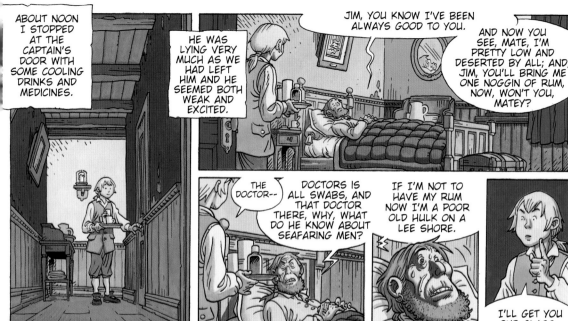

THE DOCTOR--

DOCTORS IS ALL SWABS, AND THAT DOCTOR THERE, WHY, WHAT DO HE KNOW ABOUT SEAFARING MEN?

IF I'M NOT TO HAVE MY RUM NOW I'M A POOR OLD HULK ON A LEE SHORE.

I'LL GET YOU ONE GLASS, AND NO MORE.

JIM, YOU SAW THAT SEAFARING MAN TODAY!

BLACK DOG?

AH! BLACK DOG! HE'S A BAD 'UN, BUT THERE'S WORSE THAT PUT HIM ON.

IT'S MY OLD SEA CHEST THEY'RE AFTER.

I WAS FIRST MATE, I WAS, OLD FLINT'S FIRST MATE, AND I'M THE ON'Y ONE AS KNOWS THE PLACE. HE GAVE IT ME AT SAVANNAH, WHEN HE LAY A-DYING, LIKE AS IF I WAS TO NOW, YOU SEE.

THAT'S A SUMMONS, MATE. I'LL TELL YOU IF THEY GET THAT.

ALL OLD FLINT'S CREW, ALL ON 'EM THAT'S LEFT.

BUT YOU WON'T PEACH UNLESS THEY GET THE BLACK SPOT ON ME OR UNLESS YOU SEE THAT BLACK DOG AGAIN, OR A SEAFARING MAN WITH ONE LEG, JIM--HIM ABOVE ALL.

BUT WHAT IS THE BLACK SPOT, CAPTAIN?

BUT YOU KEEP YOUR WEATHER EYE OPEN, JIM, AND I'LL SHARE WITH YOU EQUALS, UPON MY HONOR.

MY POOR FATHER DIED QUITE SUDDENLY THAT EVENING, WHICH PUT ALL OTHER MATTERS ON ONE SIDE.

OUR NATURAL DIS TRESS, THE VISIT? OF THE NEIGHBOR? THE ARRANGING O? THE FUNERAL, AND ALL THE WORK OF THE INN KEPT ME SO BUSY THAT I HAD SCARCELY TIME TO THINK OF THE CAPTAIN.

THE DAY AFTER THE FUNERAL, AND ABOUT THREE O'CLOCK, I WAS STANDING AT THE DOOR FOR A MOMENT, FULL OF SAD THOUGHTS ABOUT MY FATHER, WHEN I SAW SOMEONE DRAWING SLOWLY NEAR ALONG THE ROAD.

I NEVER SAW IN MY LIFE A MORE DREADFUL-LOOKING FIGURE.

TAP TAP TAP TAP TAP

WILL ANY KIND FRIEND INFORM A POOR BLIND MAN, WHO HAS LOST THE PRECIOUS SIGHT OF HIS EYES IN THE GRACIOUS DEFENSE OF HIS NATIVE COUNTRY, AND GOD BLESS KING GEORGE! WHERE OR IN WHAT PART OF THIS COUNTRY HE MAY NOW BE?

YOU'RE AT THE ADMIRAL BENBOW, BLACK HILL COVE, MY GOOD MAN.

WILL YOU GIVE ME YOUR HAND, MY KIND, YOUNG FRIEND, AND LEAD ME IN?

HEY?!

NOW, BOY, TAKE ME IN TO THE CAPTAIN.

SIR, I DARE NOT.

OH, *THAT'S IT!* TAKE ME IN STRAIGHT, OR I'LL BREAK YOUR ARM.

OW!

LEAD ME STRAIGHT UP TO HIM, AND WHEN I'M IN VIEW, CRY OUT, "HERE'S A FRIEND FOR YOU, BILL." IF YOU DON'T, I'LL DO THIS.

ARRG!

HERE'S A FRIEND FOR YOU, BILL.

NOW, BILL, SIT WHERE YOU ARE.

IF I CAN'T SEE, I CAN HEAR A FINGER STIRRING.

BUSINESS IS BUSINESS.

HOLD OUT YOUR LEFT HAND. BOY, TAKE HIS LEFT HAND BY THE WRIST AND BRING IT NEAR TO MY RIGHT.

AND NOW THAT'S DONE.

TAP TAP
TAP
TAP

TEN O'CLOCK! SIX HOURS.

WE'LL DO THEM YET.

GGRRR

I HAD CERTAINLY NEVER LIKED THE MAN, THOUGH OF LATE I HAD BEGUN TO PITY HIM, BUT AS SOON AS I SAW THAT HE WAS DEAD I BURST INTO A FLOOD OF TEARS.

IT WAS THE SECOND DEATH I HAD KNOWN, AND THE SORROW OF THE FIRST WAS STILL FRESH IN MY HEART.

I LOST NO TIME, OF COURSE, IN TELLING MY MOTHER ALL THAT I KNEW, AND WE SAW OURSELVES AT ONCE IN A DIFFICULT AND DANGEROUS POSITION.

SOME OF THE MAN'S MONEY WAS CERTAINLY DUE TO US, BUT IT WAS NOT LIKELY THAT OUR CAPTAIN'S SHIPMATES WOULD BE INCLINED TO GIVE UP THEIR BOOTY IN PAYMENT OF A DEAD MAN'S DEBTS.

WE RESOLVED TO GO SEEK HELP IN THE NEIGHBORING HAMLET AND WE RAN OUT IN THE GATHERING EVENING AND THE FROSTY FOG.

IT WAS ALREADY CANDLELIGHT WHEN WE REACHED THE HAMLET, AND I SHALL NEVER FORGET HOW MUCH I WAS CHEERED TO SEE THE YELLOW SHINE IN DOORS AND WINDOWS.

OUAH
OUAH

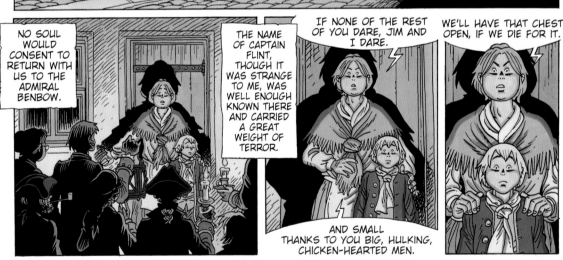

NO SOUL WOULD CONSENT TO RETURN WITH US TO THE ADMIRAL BENBOW.

THE NAME OF CAPTAIN FLINT, THOUGH IT WAS STRANGE TO ME, WAS WELL ENOUGH KNOWN THERE AND CARRIED A GREAT WEIGHT OF TERROR.

IF NONE OF THE REST OF YOU DARE, JIM AND I DARE.

AND SMALL THANKS TO YOU BIG, HULKING, CHICKEN-HEARTED MEN.

WE'LL HAVE THAT CHEST OPEN, IF WE DIE FOR IT.

ALL THEY WOULD DO WAS TO GIVE ME A LOADED PISTOL AND PROMISED TO HAVE HORSES READY SADDLED, IN CASE WE WERE PURSUED, WHILE ONE LAD WAS TO RIDE FORWARD TO THE DOCTOR'S IN SEARCH OF ARMED ASSISTANCE.

MY HEART WAS BEATING FINELY WHEN WE TWO SET FORTH IN THE COLD NIGHT.

A FULL MOON WAS BEGINNING TO RISE AND PEERED REDLY THROUGH THE UPPER EDGES OF THE FOG.

WE SLIPPED ALONG THE HEDGES, NOISELESS AND SWIFT, TILL, TO OUR RELIEF, THE DOOR OF THE ADMIRAL BENBOW HAD CLOSED BEHIND US.

TCHA CLAK

AND NOW WE HAVE TO GET THE KEY OFF *THAT*; AND WHO'S TO TOUCH IT, I SHOULD LIKE TO KNOW!

HE HAD TILL TEN, MOTHER.

You have till ten tonight.

DON DONG DOING DONG DONG DONG D

GIVE ME THE KEY.

OOOUUIIIKK

CLING CLING

I'LL SHOW THOSE ROGUES THAT I'M AN HONEST WOMAN. I'LL HAVE MY DUES, AND NOT A FARTHING OVER.

WIIK WIIIK

MOTHER, TAKE THE WHOLE, AND LET'S BE GOING.

AND I'LL TAKE THIS TO SQUARE THE COUNT.

NEXT MOMENT WE WERE BOTH GROPING DOWNSTAIRS, WE HAD OPENED THE DOOR AND WERE IN FULL RETREAT.

WE HAD NOT STARTED A MOMENT TOO SOON, FOR THE SOUND OF SEVERAL FOOTSTEPS CAME ALREADY TO OUR EARS AND WE SAW A LIGHT TOSSING TO AND FRO AND RAPIDLY ADVANCING.

WE WERE JUST AT THE LITTLE BRIDGE, SO THERE WE HAD TO STAY-- MY MOTHER ALMOST ENTIRELY EXPOSED AND BOTH OF US WITHIN EARSHOT OF THE INN.

MY CURIOSITY WAS STRONGER THAN MY FEAR, FOR I COULD NOT REMAIN WHERE I WAS, BUT CREPT BACK TO THE BANK AGAIN.

DOWN WITH THE DOOR!

AYE, AYE, SIR!

IT'S NOT CLOSED!

IN, IN, IN!

IN WITH YOU! WHY DO YOU DELAY?!

AH!

BILL'S DEAD!

SEARCH HIM, SOME OF YOU SHIRKING LUBBERS!

AND THE REST OF YOU ALOFT AND GET THE CHEST!

PEW, THEY'VE BEEN BEFORE US. SOMEONE'S TURNED THE CHEST OUT ALOW AND ALOFT.

AAAA! IS IT THERE?

THE MONEY'S THERE.

FLINT'S FIST, I MEAN!

WE DON'T SEE IT HERE NOHOW.

IT'S THESE PEOPLE OF THE INN IT'S THAT BOY.

I WISH I HAD PUT HIS EYES OUT!

THEY WERE HERE NO TIME AGO--THEY HAD THE DOOR BOLTED WHEN I TRIED IT.

SCATTER LAD, AND FIND 'EM.

THEN THERE FOLLOWED A GREAT TO-DO THROUGH ALL OUR OLD INN, FURNITURE THROWN OVER, DOORS KICKED IN, UNTIL THE VERY ROCKS RE-ECHOED.

THERE'S DIRK AGAIN. TWICE! WE'LL HAVE TO BUDGE, MATES.

BUDGE, YOU SKULK! BAND OF COWARDS! THEY CAN'T BE FAR; YOU HAVE YOUR HANDS ON IT. SCATTER AND LOOK FOR THEM, DOGS! OH, SHIVER MY SOUL, IF I HAD MY EYES!

YOU HAVE YOUR HANDS ON THOUSANDS, YOU FOOLS, AND YOU HANG A LEG! YOU'D BE AS RICH AS KINGS IF YOU COULD FIND IT!

HANG IT, PEW, WE'VE GOT THE DOUBLOONS! DON'T STAND HERE SQUALLING.

I SOON SAW WHAT THEY WERE. ONE WAS A LAD THAT HAD GONE FROM THE HAMLET TO DR. LIVESEY'S; THE REST WERE REVENUE OFFICERS, WHOM HE HAD MET BY THE WAY AND WITH WHOM HE HAD HAD THE INTELLIGENCE TO RETURN AT ONCE.

HELLO!!

TO THAT CIRCUMSTANCE MY MOTHER AND I OWED OUR PRESERVATION FROM DEATH.

PEW WAS DEAD, STONE DEAD.

WE CARRIED MY MOTHER UP TO THE HAMLET WHILE SUPERVISOR DANCE RODE ON TO KITT'S HOLE.

HIS MEN HAD TO DISMOUNT AND GROPE DOWN THE DINGLE, LEADING, AND SOMETIMES SUPPORTING, THEIR HORSES, AND IN CONTINUAL FEAR OF AMBUSHES.

BUT THE LUGGER WAS ALREADY UNDERWAY, THOUGH STILL CLOSE IN, WHEN THEY GOT DOWN TO THE HOLE.

HEY! THE SHIP! CAN YOU HEAR ME?

WE HEAR YOU! AND YOU'D BEST KEEP OUT OF THE MOONLIGHT OR YOU'LL GET SOME LEAD IN YOU!!

KA BLAM

SOON AFTER, THE LUGGER DOUBLED THE POINT AND DISAPPEARED.

I WENT BACK WITH HIM TO THE ADMIRAL BENBOW, AND YOU CANNOT IMAGINE A HOUSE IN SUCH A STATE OF SMASH.

I BELIEVE I HAVE A THING IN MY POCKET THAT THEY WERE AFTER AND, TO TELL YOU THE TRUTH, I SHOULD LIKE TO GET IT PUT IN SAFETY.

AND THOUGH NOTHING HAD ACTUALLY BEEN TAKEN AWAY EXCEPT THE CAPTAIN'S MONEYBAG AND A LITTLE SILVER FROM THE TILL, I COULD SEE AT ONCE THAT WE WERE RUINED.

TO BE SURE, BOY; QUITE RIGHT. I'LL TAKE IT, IF YOU LIKE.

I THOUGHT, PERHAPS, DR. LIVESEY

PERFECTLY RIGHT, PERFECTLY RIGHT.

AND, NOW I COME TO THINK OF IT, I MIGHT AS WELL RIDE ROUND THERE MYSELF AND REPORT TO HIM OR THE SQUIRE.

THE SUPERVISOR GAVE THE WORD, AND THE PARTY STRUCK OUT AT A BOUNCING TROT ON THE ROAD TO DR. LIVESEY'S HOUSE.

THE HOUSE WAS ALL DARK TO THE FRONT. MR. DANCE TOLD ME TO JUMP DOWN AND KNOCK. A MAID INFORMED US THAT HE HAD GONE UP TO THE HALL TO DINE AND PASS THE EVENING WITH THE SQUIRE.

THIS TIME, I RAN TO THE LODGE GATES AND UP THE LONG AVENUE TO WHERE THE WHITE LINE OF THE HALL BUILDINGS LOOKED ON EITHER HAND ON GREAT, OLD GARDENS.

COME IN, MR. DANCE.

GOOD EVENING, DANCE. AND GOOD EVENING TO YOU, FRIEND JIM. WHAT GOOD WIND BRINGS YOU HERE?

THE SUPERVISOR TOLD HIS STORY LIKE A LESSON.

LONG BEFORE IT WAS DONE, MR. TRELAWNEY HAD GOT UP AND WAS STRIDING ABOUT THE ROOM, AND THE DOCTOR, AS IF TO HEAR BETTER, HAD TAKEN OFF HIS POWDERED WIG.

MR. DANCE, YOU ARE A VERY NOBLE FELLOW.

THIS LAD HAWKINS IS A TRUMP, I PERCEIVE.

AND SO, JIM, YOU HAVE THE THING THEY WERE AFTER, HAVE YOU?

HERE IT IS, SIR.

SQUIRE, I MEAN TO KEEP JIM HAWKINS HERE TO SLEEP AT MY HOUSE AND, WITH YOUR PERMISSION, I PROPOSE WE SHOULD LET HIM SUP.

I MADE A HEARTY SUPPER, FOR I WAS A HUNGRY AS A HAWK, WHILE MR. DANCE WAS FURTHER COMPLIMENTED AND AT LAST DISMISSED.

AND NOW SQUIRE...

AND NOW, LIVESEY...

ONE AT A TIME, ONE AT A TIME! YOU HAVE HEARD OF THIS FLINT, I SUPPOSE?

HEARD OF HIM!

BLACK-BEARD WAS A CHILD TO FLINT.

THE SPANIARDS WERE SO AFRAID OF HIM THAT I TELL YOU I WAS SOMETIMES PROUD HE WAS AN ENGLISHMAN.

I'VE SEEN HIS TOPSAILS WITH THESE EYES, OFF TRINIDAD, AND THE COWARDLY SON OF A RUM-PUNCHEON THAT I SAILED WITH PUT BACK INTO PORT-OF-SPAIN.

SUPPOSING THAT I HAVE HERE IN MY HANDS SOME CLUE TO WHERE FLINT BURIED HIS TREASURE, WILL THAT TREASURE AMOUNT TO MUCH?

AMOUNT, SIR!

IF WE HAVE THE CLUE YOU TALK ABOUT, I'LL FIT OUT A SHIP IN BRISTOL DOCK AND TAKE YOU AND HAWKINS HERE ALONG WITH ME IN SEARCH OF THAT TREASURE.

VERY WELL. NOW THEN, IF JIM IS AGREEABLE, WE'LL OPEN THE PACKET.

IT CONTAINED TWO THINGS--A BOOK AND A SEALED PAPER.

FIRST OF ALL WE'LL TRY THE BOOK.

ON THE FIRST PAGE THERE WERE ONLY SOME SCRAPS OF WRITING.

THE RECORD LASTED OVER NEARLY TWENTY YEARS, THE AMOU OF THE SEPARAT ENTRIES GROWIN(LARGER AS TIME WHEN ON, AND A' THE END A GRANI TOTAL HAD BEEN MADE OUT, AND THESE WORDS APPENDED, "BONES, HIS PILE.

THE NEXT TEN OR TWELVE PAGES WERE FILLED WITH A CURIOUS SERIES OF ENTRIES. THERE WAS A DATE AT ONE END OF THE LINE AND AT THE OTHER A SUM OF MONEY, ONLY A VARYING NUMBER OF CROSSES BETWEEN THE TWO.

I CAN'T MAKE HEAD OR TAIL OF THIS.

THE THING IS AS CLEAR AS NOONDAY. THIS IS THE BLACKHEARTED HOUND'S ACCOUNT BOOK.

THESE CROSSES STAND FOR THE NAMES OF SHIPS OR TOWNS THAT THEY SANK OR PLUNDERED.

"OFFE CARACCAS," NOW; YOU SEE, HERE WAS SOME UNHAPPY VESSEL BOARDED OFF THAT COAST.

GOD HELP THE POOR SOULS THAT MANNED HER.

RIGHT! RIGHT! AND THE AMOUNTS INCREASE, YOU SEE, AS HE ROSE IN RANK.

AND NOW FOR THE OTHER.

THE PAPER HAD BEEN SEALED IN SEVERAL PLACES WITH A THIMBLE BY WAY OF SEAL.

THE DOCTOR OPENED THE SEALS WITH GREAT CARE, AND THERE FELL OUT...

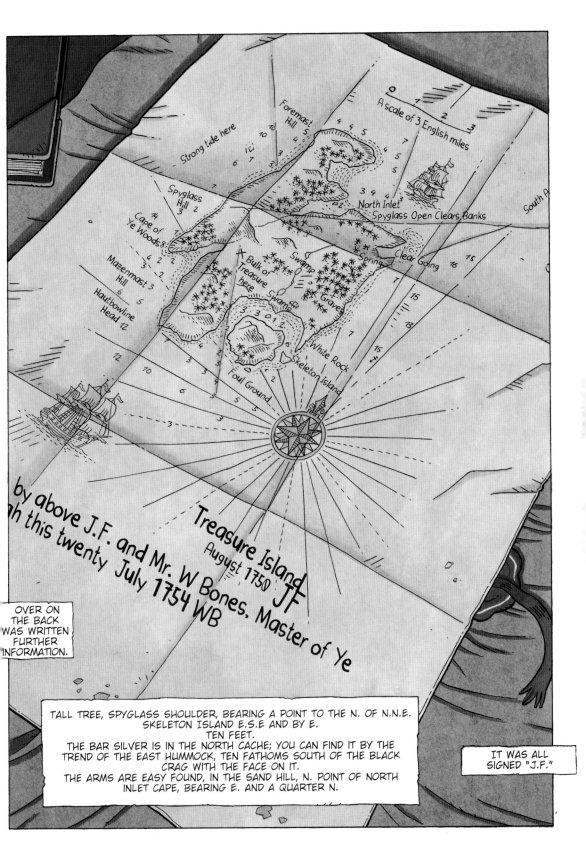

OVER ON THE BACK WAS WRITTEN FURTHER INFORMATION.

TALL TREE, SPYGLASS SHOULDER, BEARING A POINT TO THE N. OF N.N.E.
SKELETON ISLAND E.S.E AND BY E.
TEN FEET.
THE BAR SILVER IS IN THE NORTH CACHE; YOU CAN FIND IT BY THE
TREND OF THE EAST HUMMOCK, TEN FATHOMS SOUTH OF THE BLACK
CRAG WITH THE FACE ON IT.
THE ARMS ARE EASY FOUND, IN THE SAND HILL, N. POINT OF NORTH
INLET CAPE, BEARING E. AND A QUARTER N.

IT WAS ALL SIGNED "J.F."

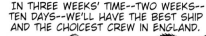

IN THREE WEEKS' TIME--TWO WEEKS-- TEN DAYS--WE'LL HAVE THE BEST SHIP AND THE CHOICEST CREW IN ENGLAND.

HAWKINS SHALL COME AS CABIN BOY.

YOU, LIVESEY, ARE SHIP'S DOCTOR.

I AM ADMIRAL.

LIVESEY, YOU WILL GIVE UP THIS WRETCHED PRACTICE AT ONCE. TOMOR- ROW I START FOR BRISTOL.

WE'LL TAKE REDRUTH, JOYCE, AND HUNTER.

WE'LL HAVE FAVORABLE WINDS, A QUICK PASSAGE, AND NOT THE LEAST DIFFICULTY IN FINDING THE SPOT, AND MONEY TO EAT--TO ROLL IN--TO PLAY DUCK AND DRAKE WITH EVER AFTER.

TRELAWNEY, I'LL GO WITH YOU, AND SO WILL JIM.

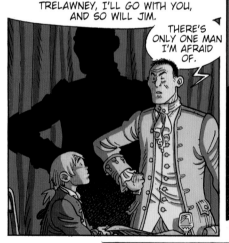

THERE'S ONLY ONE MAN I'M AFRAID OF.

AND WHO'S THAT? NAME THE DOG, SIR!

YOU!

FOR YOU CANNOT HOLD YOUR TONGUE.

WE ARE NOT THE ONLY MEN WHO KNOW OF THIS PAPER.

THESE FELLOWS WHO ATTACKED THE INN TONIGHT AND MORE, I DARE SAY, ARE ONE AND ALL BOUND THAT THEY'LL GET THAT MONEY.

WE MUST NONE OF US GO ALONE TILL WE GET TO SEA, AND, FROM FIRST TO LAST, NOT ONE OF US MUST BREATHE A WORD OF WHAT WE'VE FOUND.

LIVESEY, YOU ARE ALWAYS IN THE RIGHT OF IT. I'LL BE AS SILENT AS THE GRAVE.

IT WAS LONGER THAN THE SQUIRE IMAGINED ERE WE WERE READY FOR THE SEA.

THE DOCTOR HAD TO GO TO LONDON FOR A PHYSICIAN TO TAKE CHARGE OF HIS PRACTICE; THE SQUIRE WAS HARD AT WORK AT BRISTOL; AND I LIVED ON AT THE HALL UNDER THE PROTECTION OF OLD REDRUTH, THE GAMEKEEPER...

...ALMOST A PRISONER, BUT FULL OF SEA DREAMS OF STRANGE ISLANDS AND ADVENTURES.

I BROODED BY THE HOUR TOGETHER OVER THE MAP, ALL THE DETAILS OF WHICH I WELL REMEMBERED.

SO THE WEEKS PASSED ON, TILL ONE FINE DAY THERE CAME A LETTER.

OLD ANCHOR INN, BRISTOL, MARCH 1, 17--.

THE MOST REMARKABLE STROKE OF LUCK BROUGHT ME THE VERY MAN THAT I REQUIRED. HE WAS AN OLD SAILOR, KEPT A PUBLIC HOUSE, KNEW ALL THE SEAFARING MEN IN BRISTOL.

THE SHIP IS BOUGHT AND FITTED-- TWO HUNDRED TONS; NAME, HISPANIOLA. IT WAS THE CREW THAT TROUBLED ME.

I ENGAGED HIM ON THE SPOT TO BE SHIP'S COOK. LONG JOHN SILVER, HE IS CALLED, AND HAS LOST A LEG. BETWEEN SILVER AND MYSELF WE GOT TOGETHER IN A FEW DAYS A COMPANY OF THE TOUGHEST SALTS IMAGINABLE.

SO NOW, LIVESEY, COME POST; DO NOT LOSE AN HOUR.

LET YOUNG HAWKINS GO AT ONCE TO SEE HIS MOTHER, WITH REDRUTH FOR A GUARD; AND THEN BOTH COME FULL SPEED TO BRISTOL.

Long John Silver
Between Silver an
myself we in a few da
a company of the
So now, Livesey, come pos
do Hawkins so at once
to see his For a guard;
and then both come
To Bristol.

— John Trelawney

JOHN TRELAWNEY.

THE NEXT MORNING HE AND I SET OUT FOR THE ADMIRAL BENBOW.

I FOUND MY MOTHER IN GOOD HEALTH AND SPIRITS.

THE SQUIRE HAD HAD EVERYTHING REPAIRED, AND THE PUBLIC ROOM AND THE SIGN REPAINTED.

HE HAD FOUND HER A BOY AS APPRENTICE ALSO, TO HELP WHILE I WAS GONE.

THE NIGHT PASSED, AND THE NEXT DAY, AFTER DINNER, REDRUTH AND I WERE AGAIN ON THE ROAD.

I SAID GOODBYE TO MOTHER AND THE COVE WHERE I HAD LIVED SINCE I WAS BORN, AND THE DEAR OLD ADMIRAL BENBOW.

ONE OF MY LAST THOUGHTS WAS OF THE CAPTAIN, WHO HAD SO OFTEN STRODE ALONG THE BEACH WITH HIS COCKED HAT, HIS SABER-CUT CHEEK, AND HIS OLD BRASS TELESCOPE.

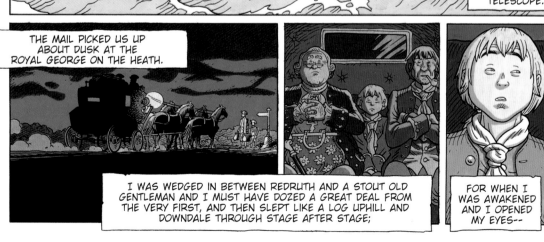

THE MAIL PICKED US UP ABOUT DUSK AT THE ROYAL GEORGE ON THE HEATH.

I WAS WEDGED IN BETWEEN REDRUTH AND A STOUT OLD GENTLEMAN AND I MUST HAVE DOZED A GREAT DEAL FROM THE VERY FIRST, AND THEN SLEPT LIKE A LOG UPHILL AND DOWNDALE THROUGH STAGE AFTER STAGE;

FOR WHEN I WAS AWAKENED AND I OPENED MY EYES--

BRISTOL, GET DOWN.

WHERE ARE WE?

MR. TRELAWNEY HAD TAKEN UP RESIDENCE AT AN INN FAR DOWN THE DOCKS, TO SUPERINTEND THE WORK UPON THE SCHOONER.

THITHER WE HAD NOW TO WALK, AND OUR WAY, TO MY GREAT DELIGHT, LAY BESIDE THE MULTITUDE OF SHIPS OF ALL SIZES AND RIGS AND NATIONS.

THOUGH I HAD LIVED BY THE SHORE ALL MY LIFE, I SEEMED NEVER TO HAVE BEEN NEAR THE SEA TILL THEN.

I SAW THE MOST WONDERFUL FIGUREHEADS THAT HAD ALL BEEN FAR OVER THE OCEAN.

I SAW, BESIDES, MANY OLD SAILORS, WITH RINGS IN THEIR EARS, AND WHISKERS CURLED IN RINGLETS, AND TARRY PIGTAILS, AND THEIR SWAGGERING, CLUMSY SEAWALK.

AND I WAS GOING TO SEA MYSELF; TO SEA IN A SCHOONER WITH ALL ITS CREW; BOUND FOR AN UNKNOWN ISLAND, AND TO SEEK FOR BURIED TREASURES!

HERE YOU ARE!

AND THE DOCTOR CAME LAST NIGHT FROM LONDON. BRAVO! THE SHIP'S COMPANY COMPLETE!

OH, SIR, WHEN DO WE SAIL?

SAIL! WE SAIL TOMORROW!

WHEN I HAD DONE BREAKFASTING, THE SQUIRE GAVE ME A NOTE ADDRESSED TO JOHN SILVER, AT THE SIGN OF THE SPYGLASS, A LITTLE TAVERN WITH A LARGE BRASS TELESCOPE FOR SIGN.

I SET OFF, OVERJOYED AT THIS OPPORTUNITY TO SEE SOME MORE OF THE SHIPS AND SEAMEN.

IT WAS A WELCOMING PLACE.

THE CUSTOMERS WERE MOSTLY SEAFARING MEN AND THEY TALKED SO LOUDLY THAT I HUNG AT THE DOOR, ALMOST AFRAID TO ENTER.

AS I WAS WAITING, A MAN CAME OUT OF A SIDE ROOM AND, AT A GLANCE, I WAS SURE HE MUST BE LONG JOHN.

FROM THE VERY FIRST MENTION OF LONG JOHN IN SQUIRE TRELAWNEY'S LETTER, I HAD TAKEN A FEAR IN MY MIND THAT HE MIGHT BE THE VERY ONE-LEGGED SAILOR WHOM I HAD WATCHED FOR SO LONG AT THE OLD BENBOW.

BUT ONE LOOK AT THE MAN BEFORE ME WAS ENOUGH; I THOUGHT I KNEW WHAT A BUCCANEER WAS LIKE--A VERY DIFFERENT CREATURE, ACCORDING TO ME, FROM THIS PLEASANT-TEMPERED LANDLORD.

I PLUCKED UP COURAGE AT ONCE, CROSSED THE THRESHOLD, AND WALKED UP RIGHT UP TO THE MAN.

MR. SILVER, SIR?

YES, MY LAD, SUCH IS MY NAME. AND WHO MAY YOU BE?

OH! I SEE. YOU ARE OUR NEW CABIN BOY, EH? PLEASED I AM TO MEET YOU.

OH, STOP HIM! IT'S BLACK DOG!

I DON'T CARE TWO COPPERS WHO HE IS, BUT HE HASN'T PAID HIS SCORE!

HARRY, BEN, RUN AND CATCH HIM.

WHO DID YOU SAY HE WAS? BLACK WHAT?

DOG, SIR. HAS MR. TRELAWNEY NOT TOLD YOU OF THE BUCCANEERS? HE WAS ONE OF THEM.

BLACK DOG? NO, I DON'T KNOW THE NAME, NOT I.

YET I KIND OF THINK I'VE--YES, I'VE SEEN THE SWAB. HE USED TO COME HERE WITH A BLIND BEGGAR.

YOU MAY BE SURE. I KNEW THAT BLIND MAN. HIS NAME WAS PEW.

IT WAS! PEW! THAT WERE HIS NAME FOR CERTAIN. AH, HE LOOKED A SHARK, HE DID!

MY SUSPICIONS HAD BEEN THOROUGHLY REAWAKENED ON FINDING BLACK DOG, AND I WATCHED THE COOK NARROWLY.

BUT HE WAS TOO DEEP AND TOO READY AND TOO CLEVER FOR ME, AND BY THE TIME THE TWO MEN HAD COME BACK AND CONFESSED THAT THEY HAD LOST THE TRACK IN A CROWD, I WOULD HAVE GONE BAIL FOR THE INNOCENCE OF LONG JOHN SILVER.

THERE'S CAP'N TRELAWNEY WHAT'S HE TO THINK? HERE I HAVE THIS CONFOUNDED SON OF A DUTCHMAN SITTING IN MY OWN HOUSE DRINKING OF MY OWN RUM!

WHEN I WAS AN A.B. MASTER MARINER I'D HAVE COME UP ALONGSIDE OF HIM AND BROACHED HIM TO IN A BRACE OF OLD SHAKES, I WOULD; BUT NOW--

SO, ENOUGH OF ALL THAT.

I'LL PUT ON MY OLD COCKED HAT AND STEP ALONG OF YOU TO REPORT THIS HERE AFFAIR TO CAP'N TRELAWNEY.

ON OUR LITTLE WALK ALONG THE QUAYS HE MADE HIMSELF THE MOST INTEREST-ING COMPANION, TELLING ME ABOUT THE DIFFERENT SHIPS THAT WE PASSED BY, THEIR RIG, TONNAGE, AND NATIONALITY

EVERY NOW AND THEN TELLING ME SOME LITTLE ANECDOTE OF SHIPS OR SEAMEN, OR REPEATING A NAUTICAL PHRASE TILL I HAD LEARNED IT PERFECTLY.

I BEGAN TO SEE THAT HERE WAS ONE OF THE BEST OF POSSIBLE SHIPMATES.

WHEN WE GOT TO THE INN, LONG JOHN TOLD THE STORY FROM FIRST TO LAST, WITH A GREAT DEAL OF SPIRIT AND THE MOST PERFECT TRUTH.

THEN, AFTER HE HAD BEEN COM-PLIMENTED, LONG JOHN TOOK UP HIS CRUTCH AND DEPARTED.

WELL, SQUIRE, I DON'T PUT MUCH FAITH IN YOUR DISCOVERIES, AS A GENERAL THING, BUT THIS JOHN SILVER SUITS ME.

THE MAN'S A TRUMP.

AND NOW, JIM MAY COME ON BOARD WITH US, MAY HE NOT?

TO BE SURE, HE MAY.

TAKE YOUR HAT, HAWKINS, AND WE'LL SEE THE SHIP.

THE *HISPANIOLA* LAY SOME WAY OUT, AND WE WENT OUT UNDER THE FIGUREHEADS AND ROUND THE STERNS OF MANY OTHER SHIPS, AND THEIR CABLES SOMETIMES GRATED UNDERNEATH OUR KEEL AND SOMETIMES SWUNG ABOVE US.

AT LAST, HOWEVER, WE GOT ALONGSIDE AND WERE MET AND SALUTED BY THE MATE, MR. ARROW, A BROWN OLD SAILOR WITH EARRINGS IN HIS EARS AND A SQUINT.

HE AND THE SQUIRE WERE VERY THICK AND FRIENDLY, BUT I SOON OBSERVED THAT THINGS WERE NOT THE SAME BETWEEN MR. TRELAWNEY AND THE CAPTAIN.

CAPTAIN SMOLLETT, SIR, AXING TO SPEAK WITH YOU.

I AM ALWAYS AT THE CAPTAIN'S ORDERS. SHOW HIM IN.

WELL, SIR, BETTER SPEAK PLAIN.

I DON'T LIKE THIS CRUISE; I DON'T LIKE THE MEN; AND I DON'T LIKE MY OFFICER. THAT'S SHORT AND SWEET.

POSSIBLY, SIR, YOU MAY NOT LIKE YOUR EMPLOYER EITHER?

GENTLEMEN, I BEG YOU!

YOU DON'T, YOU SAY, LIKE THIS CRUISE. NOW, WHY?

I LEARNED WE ARE GOING AFTER TREASURE HEARD IT FROM MY OWN HANDS.

HISPANIOLA

I DON'T LIKE TREASURE VOYAGES. I DON'T LIKE THEM, ABOVE ALL, WHEN THEY ARE SECRET, AND THAT SECRET IS KNOWN TO ALL.

IT'S MY BELIEF NEITHER OF YOU GENTLEMEN KNOW WHAT YOU ARE ABOUT; BUT I'LL TELL YOU MY WAY OF IT--LIFE OR DEATH, AND A CLOSE RUN.

WE'RE READY TO TAKE THE RISK. AND DON'T WORRY; WE ARE NOT SO IGNORANT AS YOU BELIEVE US. TELL US WHAT YOU WANT.

VERY GOOD. THE MEN ARE PUTTING THE POWDER AND THE ARMS IN THE FOREHOLD. NOW YOU HAVE A GOOD PLACE UNDER THE CABIN; WHY NOT PUT THEM THERE?

NEXT, YOU ARE BRINGING FOUR OF YOUR OWN PEOPLE WITH YOU. WHY NOT GIVE THEM THE BERTHS HERE BESIDE THE CABIN?

ONE MORE THING. THERE'S BEEN TOO MUCH BLABBING ALREADY.

FAR TOO MUCH.

I'LL TELL YOU WHAT I'VE HEARD MYSELF. THAT YOU HAVE A MAP OF AN ISLAND; THAT THERE'S CROSSES ON THE MAP TO SHOW WHERE TREASURE IS. I DEMAND THAT IT SHALL BE KEPT SECRET EVEN FROM ME AND MR. ARROW. OTHERWISE I WOULD ASK YOU TO LET ME RESIGN.

YOU WISH US TO KEEP THIS MATTER DARK, AND TO MAKE A GARRISON OF THE STERN PART OF THE SHIP. IN OTHER WORDS, YOU FEAR A MUTINY.

I SEE THINGS GOING, AS I THINK, NOT QUITE RIGHT. AND I ASK YOU TO TAKE CERTAIN PRECAUTIONS, AND THAT'S ALL.

CAPTAIN SMOLLETT, WHEN YOU CAME IN HERE I'LL STAKE MY WIG YOU MEANT MORE THAN THIS.

DOCTOR, YOU ARE SMART. WHEN I CAME IN HERE I MEANT TO GET DISCHARGED. I HAD NOT THOUGHT THAT MR. TRELAWNEY WOULD HEAR A WORD.

AS IT IS, I HAVE HEARD YOU. I WILL DO AS YOU DESIRE, BUT I THINK THE WORSE OF YOU.

THAT'S AS YOU PLEASE, SIR.

YOU'LL FIND I DO MY DUTY.

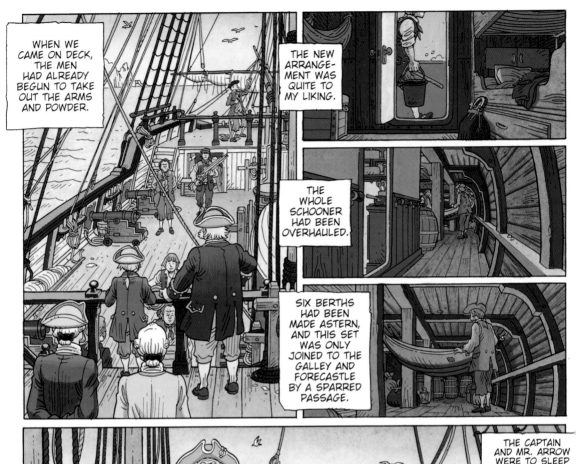

WHEN WE CAME ON DECK, THE MEN HAD ALREADY BEGUN TO TAKE OUT THE ARMS AND POWDER.

THE NEW ARRANGEMENT WAS QUITE TO MY LIKING.

THE WHOLE SCHOONER HAD BEEN OVERHAULED.

SIX BERTHS HAD BEEN MADE ASTERN, AND THIS SET WAS ONLY JOINED TO THE GALLEY AND FORECASTLE BY A SPARRED PASSAGE.

HUNTER, JOYCE, THE DOCTOR, AND THE SQUIRE OCCUPIED TWO OF THESE BERTHS; REDRUTH AND I, THE THIRD.

THE CAPTAIN AND MR. ARROW WERE TO SLEEP ON DECK IN THE COMPANION, WHICH HAD BEEN ENLARGED ON EACH SIDE TILL YOU MIGHT ALMOST HAVE CALLED IT A ROUNDHOUSE.

EVEN THE MATE SEEMED PLEASED WITH THE ARRANGEMENT.

WE WERE ALL HARD AT WORK, CHANGING THE POWDER AND THE BERTHS, WHEN THE LAST MAN OR TWO, AND LONG JOHN SILVER ALONG WITH THEM, CAME OFF IN A SHORE BOAT.

SO HO, MATES!

WHAT'S THIS?

WE'RE A-CHANGING OF THE POWDER.

WHY, BY THE POWERS, IF WE DO, WE'LL MISS THE MORNING TIDE!

MY ORDERS!

YOU MAY GO BELOW, MY MAN!

HANDS WILL WANT SUPPER.

AYE, AYE, SIR.

THAT'S A GOOD MAN, CAPTAIN.

VERY LIKELY, SIR.

HERE, YOU SHIP'S BOY! OFF WITH YOU TO THE COOK AND GET SOME WORK.

I'LL HAVE NO FAVORITES ON MY SHIP.

I ASSURE YOU I WAS QUITE OF THE SQUIRE'S WAY OF THINKING AND HATED THE CAPTAIN DEEPLY.

WE SPENT ALL THAT NIGHT PREPARING FOR OUR DEPARTURE.

BOATFULS OF THE SQUIRE'S FRIENDS CAME OFF TO WISH HIM A GOOD VOYAGE AND A SAFE RETURN.

TRRiiiii

NOW, BARBECUE, TIP US A STAVE!

THE OLD ONE!

AYE, AYE, MATES!

WE NEVER HAD A NIGHT AT THE ADMIRAL BENBOW WHEN I HAD HALF THE WORK, AND I WAS DOG-TIRED WHEN, A LITTLE BEFORE DAWN, THE BOATSWAIN SOUNDED HIS PIPE.

FIFTEEN MEN ON THE DEAD MAN'S CHEST

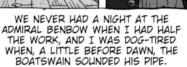

YO-HO-HO, AND A BOTTLE OF RUM!

I AM NOT GOING TO RELATE THAT VOYAGE IN DETAIL.

THE SHIP PROVED TO BE A GOOD SHIP, THE CREW WERE CAPABLE SEAMEN, AND THE CAPTAIN THOROUGHLY UNDERSTOOD HIS BUSINESS.

MR. ARROW, HOWEVER, TURNED OUT EVEN WORSE THAN THE CAPTAIN HAD FEARED.

HE HAD NO COMMAND AMONG THE MEN AND AFTER A DAY OR TWO AT SEA HE APPEARED ON DECK WITH MARKS OF DRUNKENNESS.

TIME AFTER TIME HE WAS ORDERED BELOW IN DISGRACE.

WE COULD NEVER MAKE OUT WHERE HE GOT THE DRINK. THAT WAS THE SHIP'S MYSTERY.

BUT IT WAS PLAIN THAT AT THIS RATE HE MUST SOON KILL HIMSELF.

SO NOBODY WAS MUCH SURPRISED, NOR VERY SORRY, WHEN ONE DARK NIGHT, WITH A HEAD SEA, HE DISAPPEARED ENTIRELY.

OVERBAOARD! WELL, GENTLEMEN, THAT SAVES US THE TROUBLE OF PUTTING HIM IN IRONS.

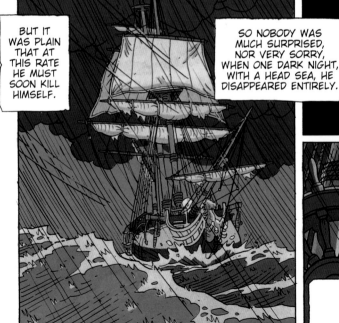

SO MR. ARROW WAS REPLACED BY JOB ANDERSON, THE BOATSWAIN, AND SECONDED BY ISRAEL HANDS, A WILY, OLD, EXPERIENCED SEAMAN.

HE WAS A GREAT CONFIDANT OF LONG JOHN SILVER, WHICH LEADS ME TO SPEAK OF OUR SHIP'S COOK, BARBECUE, AS THE MEN CALLED HIM.

IT WAS SOMETHING TO SEE HIM PROP HIMSELF THEN, YIELDING TO EVERY MOVE-MENT OF THE SHIP, GET ON WITH HIS COOKING LIKE SOMEONE SAFE ASHORE.

HE WOULD HAND HIMSELF FROM ONE PLACE TO ANOTHER, NOW USING THE CRUTCH, NOW TRAILING IT ALONGSIDE BY THE LANYARD, AS QUICKLY AS ANOTHER MAN COULD WALK.

HE'S NO COMMON MAN, BARBECUE. HE HAD GOOD SCHOOLING AND CAN SPEAK LIKE A BOOK WHEN SO MINDED.

A LION'S NOTHING ALONGSIDE OF LONG JOHN! I SEEN HIM GRAPPLE FOUR, AND KNOCK THEIR HEADS TOGETHER--HIM UNARMED.

ALL THE CREW RESPECTED AND EVEN OBEYED HIM.

COME AWAY, HAWKINS, COME AND HAVE A YARN WITH JOHN. NOBODY MORE WELCOME, MY SON.

HERE'S CAP'N FLINT, PREDICTING SUCCESS TO OUR V'YAGE WASN'T YOU, CAP'N?

TO ME HE WAS UNWEARIEDLY KIND AND ALWAYS GLAD TO SEE ME IN THE GALLEY, WHICH HE KEPT AS CLEAN AS A NEW PIN.

PIECES OF EIGHT! PIECES OF EIGHT!

NOW, THAT BIRD IS MAYBE TWO HUNDRED YEARS OLD, HAWKINS. SHE'S SAILED WITH ENGLAND THE PIRATE. SHE'S BEEN AT MADAGASCAR, AND AT MALABAR, AND SURINAM, AND PROVIDENCE, AND PORTOBELLO.

AH, SHE'S A HANDSOME CRAFT, SHE IS.

THE BIRD WOULD PECK AT THE BARS AND SWEAR STRAIGHT ON, PASSING BELIEF FOR WICKEDNESS.

THERE, YOU CAN'T TOUCH PITCH AND NOT BE MUCKED, LAD. THIS POOR OLD INNOCENT BIRD O' MINE SWEARING BLUE FIRE AND NONE THE WISER.

IN THE MEANTIME, THE SQUIRE AND CAPTAIN SMOLLETT WERE STILL ON PRETTY DISTANT TERMS WITH EACH OTHER.

THE SQUIRE DESPISED THE CAPTAIN. THE CAPTAIN, ON HIS PART, NEVER SPOKE BUT WHEN HE WAS SPOKEN TO.

HE OWNED, WHEN DRIVEN INTO A CORNER, THAT HE SEEMED TO BE WRONG ABOUT THE CREW, AND ALL HAD BEHAVED FAIRLY WELL.

AS FOR THE SHIP, HE HAD TAKEN A DOWNRIGHT FANCY TO HER.

SHE'LL LIE A POINT NEARER THE WIND THAN A MAN HAS A RIGHT TO EXPECT OF HIS OWN MARRIED WIFE.

BUT, ALL I SAY IS WE'RE NOT HOME AGAIN--

AND I DON'T LIKE THIS CRUISE.

A TRIFLE MORE OF THAT MAN, AND I SHALL EXPLODE!

EVERY MAN ON BOARD SEEMED WELL CONTENT, AND IT IS MY BELIEF THERE WAS NEVER A SHIP'S COMPANY SO SPOILED SINCE NOAH PUT TO SEA.

DOUBLE GROG WAS GOING ON THE LEAST EXCUSE.

THERE WAS DUFF ON ODD DAYS AND ALWAYS A BARREL OF APPLES ON THE DECK FOR ANYONE TO HELP HIMSELF THAT HAD A FANCY.

NEVER KNEW GOOD COME OF IT YET.

SPOIL FOC'S'LE HANDS, MAKE DEVILS. THAT'S MY BELIEF.

WE HAD RUN UP THE TRADES TO GET THE WIND OF THE ISLAND WE WERE AFTER AND NOW WE WERE RUNNING DOWN FOR IT WITH A BRIGHT LOOKOUT DAY AND NIGHT.

IT WAS ABOUT THE LAST DAY OF OUR OUTWARD VOYAGE, BY THE LARGEST COMPUTATION.

SOMETIME THAT NIGHT, OR, AT THE LATEST, BEFORE NOON OF THE MORROW, WE SHOULD SIGHT THE TREASURE ISLAND. EVERYONE WAS IN THE BRAVEST SPIRITS.

NOW, JUST AFTER SUNDOWN, WHEN ALL MY WORK WAS OVER, AND I WAS ON MY WAY TO MY BERTH, IT OCCURRED TO ME THAT I SHOULD LIKE AN APPLE.

THE WATCH WAS ALL FORWARD, THE MAN AT THE HELM WAS WATCHING THE LUFF OF THE SAIL, AND THE ONLY SOUND WAS THE SWISH OF THE SEA AGAINST THE SIDES OF THE SHIPS.

IN I GOT BODILY INTO THE APPLE BARREL, AND FOUND THERE WAS SCARCE AN APPLE LEFT.

SITTING DOWN THERE IN THE DARK, WHAT WITH THE SOUND OF THE WATER AND THE ROCKING OF THE SHIP, I WAS ON THE POINT OF FALLING ASLEEP--

WHEN A HEAVY MAN SAT DOWN WITH RATHER A CLASH CLOSE BY.

IT WAS SILVER'S VOICE, AND, BEFORE I HEARD A DOZEN WORDS, I WOULD NOT HAVE SHOWN MYSELF FOR ALL THE WORLD--

FOR FROM THESE DOZEN WORDS I UNDERSTOOD THAT THE LIVES OF ALL THE HONEST MEN ABOARD DEPENDED UPON ME ALONE.

FLINT WAS CAP'N; I WAS QUARTERMASTER, ALONG OF MY TIMBER LEG.

THE SAME BROADSIDE I LOST MY LEG, OLD PEW LOST HIS DEADLIGHTS.

SO IT WAS WITH THE OLD *WALRUS*, FLINT'S OLD SHIP, AS I'VE SEEN A-MUCK WITH THE RED BLOOD AND FIT TO SINK WITH GOLD.

AH! HE WAS THE FLOWER OF THE FLOCK, WAS FLINT!

BUT NOW, YOU LOOK HERE: YOU'RE YOUNG, BUT YOU'RE AS SMART AS PAINT. I SEE THAT WHEN I SET MY EYES ON YOU, AND I'LL TALK TO YOU LIKE A MAN.

HERE IT IS ABOUT GENTLEMEN OF FORTUNE. THEY LIVES ROUGH, AND THEY RISK SWINGING, BUT THEY EAT AND DRINK LIKE FIGHTING COCKS, AND WHEN A CRUISE IS DONE, WHY IT'S HUNDREDS OF POUNDS IN THEIR POCKETS.

NOW, THE MOST GOES FOR RUM AND A GOOD FLING, AND TO SEA AGAIN IN THEIR SHIRTS.

BUT ME, I PUTS IT ALL AWAY. I'M FIFTY, AND ONCE BACK FROM THIS CRUISE, I SET UP GENTLEMAN IN EARNEST.

AND HOW DID I BEGIN? BEFORE THE MAST, LIKE YOU!

THE SPYGLASS IS SOLD, LEASE AND GOODWILL AND RIGGING; AND MY OLD MISSIS'S OFF TO MEET ME.

AND CAN YOU TRUST YOUR MISSIS?

I HAVE A WAY WITH ME, I HAVE. WHEN A MATE BRINGS A SLIP ON HIS CABLE, IT WON'T BE IN THE SAME WORLD WITH OLD JOHN.

THERE WAS SOME THAT WAS FEARED OF PEW, AND SOME THAT WAS FEARED OF FLINT; BUT FLINT HIS OWN SELF WAS FEARED OF ME.

WELL, I TELL YOU NOW, I DIDN'T HALF A QUARTER LIKE THE JOB TILL I HAD THIS TALK WITH YOU--

BUT THERE'S MY HAND ON IT NOW.

AND A BRAVE LAD YOU WERE AND SMART, TOO, AND A FINER FIGUREHEAD FOR A GENTLEMAN OF FORTUNE I NEVER CLAPPED EYES ON.

SILVER GAVE A LITTLE WHISTLE, A THIRD MAN STROLLED UP.

DICK'S SQUARE.

OH, I KNOW'D DICK WAS SQUARE. HE'S NO FOOL, IS DICK.

BUT LOOK HERE, BARBECUE, I'VE HAD A'MOST ENOUGH OF CAP'N SMOLLETT; HE'S HAZED ME LONG ENOUGH, BY THUNDER!

I WANT TO GO INTO THAT CABIN, I DO. I WANT THEIR PICKLES AND WINE AND THAT.

ISRAEL, YOUR HEAD AIN'T MUCH ACCOUNT, NOR EVER WAS. YOU'LL BERTH FORWARD AND YOU'LL LIVE HARD AND YOU'LL SPEAK SOFT AND YOU'LL KEEP SOBER--

TILL I GIVE THE WORD; AND YOU MAY LAY TO THAT, MY SON.

WHY, HOW MANY TALL SHIPS, THINK YE, NOW, HAVE I SEEN LAID ABOARD? AND HOW MANY BRISK LADS DRYING IN THE SUN AT EXECUTION DOCK?

AND ALL FOR THIS SAME HURRY AND HURRY AND HURRY. YOU HEAR ME?

IF YOU WOULD ON'Y LAY YOUR COURSE AND A P'INT TO WINDWARD, YOU WOULD RIDE IN CARRIAGES, YOU WOULD. BUT NOT YOU! I KNOW YOU. YOU'LL HAVE YOUR MOUTHFUL OF RUM TOMORROW AND GO HANG.

EVERYBODY KNOW'D YOU WAS A KIND OF CHAPLING, JOHN, BUT THERE'S OTHERS AS COULD HAND AND STEER AS WELL AS YOU.

SO? WELL, AND WHERE ARE THEY NOW?

PEW WAS THAT SORT AND DIED A BEGGARMAN. FLINT WAS AND HE DIED OF RUM AT SAVANNAH.

BUT, WHEN WE DO LAY 'EM ATHWART, WHAT ARE WE TO DO WITH 'EM, ANYHOW?

WELL, WHAT WOULD YOU THINK? PUT 'EM ASHORE LIKES MAROONS? THAT WOULD HAVE BEEN ENGLAND'S WAY. OR CUT 'EM DOWN LIKE THAT MUCH PORK? THAT WOULD HAVE BEEN FLINT'S OR BILLY BONES'S.

BILLY WAS THE MAN FOR THAT. DEAD MEN DON'T BITE, SAYS HE.

DOOTY IS DOOTY, MATES. I GIVE MY VOTE--DEATH. WAIT IS WHAT I SAY, BUT WHEN THE TIME COMES, WHY, LET HER RIP!

JOHN, YOU'RE A MAN!

ONLY ONE THING I CLAIM--I CLAIM TRELAWNEY. I'LL WRING HIS CALF'S HEAD OFF HIS BODY WITH THESE HANDS.

DICK! BE A SWEET LAD AND GET ME AN APPLE, TO WET MY PIPE LIKE.

YOU MAY FANCY THE TERROR I WAS IN!

I HEARD DICK APPROACH-ING.

BUT AT THE SAME MOMENT, THE VOICE OF HANDS--

OH, STOW THAT! LET'S HAVE A GO OF THE RUM.

DICK, I'VE A GAUGE ON THE KEG. THERE'S THE KEY; YOU FILL A PANNIKIN AND BRING IT UP.

DICK WAS GONE BUT A LITTLE WHILE, AND DURING HIS ABSENCE ISRAEL SPOKE STRAIGHT IN THE COOK'S EAR.

BESIDES OTHER SCRAPS THAT TENDED TO THE SAME PURPOSE, THIS WHOLE CLAUSE WAS AUDIBLE: "NOT ANOTHER MAN OF THEM'LL JINE."

HENCE THERE WERE STILL FAITHFUL MEN ON BOARD.

WHEN DICK RETURNED, ONE AFTER ANOTHER TOOK A PANNIKIN AND DRANK.

TO LUCK!

HERE'S TO OLD FLINT!

HERE'S TO OURSELVES, AND HOLD YOUR LUFF,

PLENTY OF PRIZES AND PLENTY OF DUFF.

JUST THEN A SORT OF BRIGHTNESS FELL UPON ME IN THE BARREL, AND, LOOKING UP, I FOUND THE MOON HAD RISEN AND WAS SHIN-ING WHITE ON THE LUFF OF THE FORESAIL.

AND ALMOST AT THE SAME TIME, THE LOOKOUT SHOUTED:

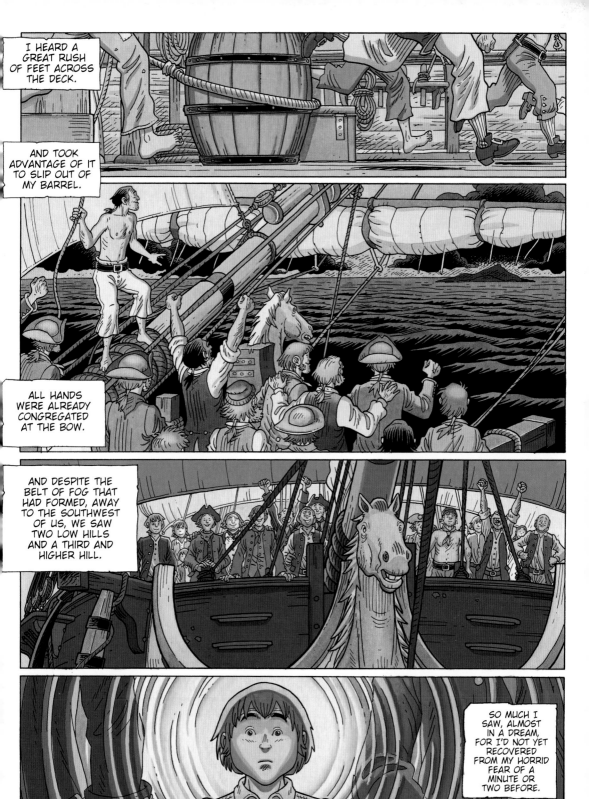

I HEARD A GREAT RUSH OF FEET ACROSS THE DECK.

AND TOOK ADVANTAGE OF IT TO SLIP OUT OF MY BARREL.

ALL HANDS WERE ALREADY CONGREGATED AT THE BOW.

AND DESPITE THE BELT OF FOG THAT HAD FORMED, AWAY TO THE SOUTHWEST OF US, WE SAW TWO LOW HILLS AND A THIRD AND HIGHER HILL.

SO MUCH I SAW, ALMOST IN A DREAM, FOR I'D NOT YET RECOVERED FROM MY HORRID FEAR OF A MINUTE OR TWO BEFORE.

AND NOW, MEN, HAS ANY ONE OF YOU EVER SEEN THAT LAND AHEAD?

I HAVE, SIR.

I'VE WATERED THERE WITH A TRADER I WAS COOK IN.

THE ANCHORAGE IS ON THE SOUTH, BEHIND AN ISLET, I FANCY?

YES, SIR; SKELETON ISLAND THEY CALLS IT.

IT WERE A MAIN PLACE FOR PIRATES ONCE. THOSE THREE HILLS ARE FOREMAST, MAIN AND MIZZEN, SIR. THE BIG 'UN IS CALLED SPYGLASS, ASKING YOUR PARDON.

I HAVE A CHART HERE. SEE IF THAT'S THE PLACE.

LONG JOHN'S EYES BURNED IN HIS HEAD AS HE TOOK THE CHART.

YES, SIR, THIS IS THE SPOT AND VERY PRETTILY DRAWED OUT. WHO MIGHT HAVE DONE THAT, I WONDER?

THANK YOU, MY MAN. YOU MAY GO.

AH, JIM, MY BOY!!

THIS ISLAND IS A SWEET SPOT FOR A LAD TO GET ASHORE ON. YOU'LL BATHE AND YOU'LL CLIMB TREES, AND YOU'LL HUNT GOATS.

WHY, IT MAKES ME YOUNG AGAIN.

JIM! COME HERE FOR A MOMENT!

YES, DOCTOR LIVESEY?

I LEFT MY PIPE BELOW, WOULD YOU BE SO KIND AS TO GO FETCH IT FOR ME?

DOCTOR, LET ME SPEAK. YOU MUST ALL GO DOWN TO THE CABIN. I HAVE TERRIBLE NEWS.

THE DOCTOR ACTED AS IF HE HAD ASKED ME A QUESTION.

THANK YOU, JIM. THAT WAS ALL I WANTED TO KNOW.

HE REJOINED THE OTHER TWO. THEY SPOKE TOGETHER, AND THEN THE CAPTAIN PIPED UP AND PROPOSED TO THE CREW TO DRINK A GROG AS A REWARD FOR THE WORK DONE DURING THE VOYAGE.

HURRAH FOR CAP'N SMOLLETT!

AFTER WHICH, WE WENT DOWN TO THE CABIN, AND AS SHORT AS I COULD MAKE IT, TOLD THE WHOLE DETAILS OF SILVER'S CONVERSATION. THEY KEPT THEIR EYES UPON MY FACE FROM FIRST TO LAST.

NOW, CAPTAIN, YOU WERE RIGHT, AND I WAS WRONG.

I OWN MYSELF AN ASS, AND I AWAIT YOUR ORDERS.

NO MORE AN ASS THAN I, SIR.

I NEVER HEARD OF A CREW THAT MEANT TO MUTINY BUT WHAT SHOWED SIGNS BEFORE.

CAPTAIN, WITH YOUR PERMISSION, THIS IS ALL THE WORK OF SILVER.

BUT THIS IS TALK; THIS DOESN'T LEAD TO ANYTHING.

FIRST POINT. WE MUST GO ON, BECAUSE WE CAN'T TURN BACK.

SECOND POINT, WE HAVE TIME BEFORE US--AT LEAST UNTIL THIS TREASURE'S FOUND.

THIRD POINT, THERE ARE FAITHFUL HANDS.

NOW, WHAT I PROPOSE IS TO COME TO BLOWS SOME FINE DAY WHEN THEY LEAST EXPECT IT. WE CAN COUNT, I TAKE IT, ON YOUR OWN HOME SERVANTS, MR. TRELAWNEY?

HISPANIOLA

AS UPON MYSELF!

THREE, OURSELVES MAKE SEVEN, COUNTING HAWKINS, HERE.

WELL, GENTLEMAN, THE BEST I CAN SAY IS THAT WE MUST LAY TO AND KEEP A BRIGHT LOOKOUT.

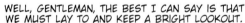

JIM HERE CAN HELP US MORE THAN ANYONE. THE MEN ARE NOT SHY WITH HIM, AND JIM IS A NOTICING LAD.

HAWKINS, I PUT PRODI-GIOUS FAITH IN YOU.

I BEGAN TO FEEL PRETTY DESPERATE AT THIS, FOR I FELT ALTOGETHER HELPLESS.

WE WERE SEVEN AGAINST NINETEEN, AND WITH A BOY, WERE WE REALLY ONLY SIX.

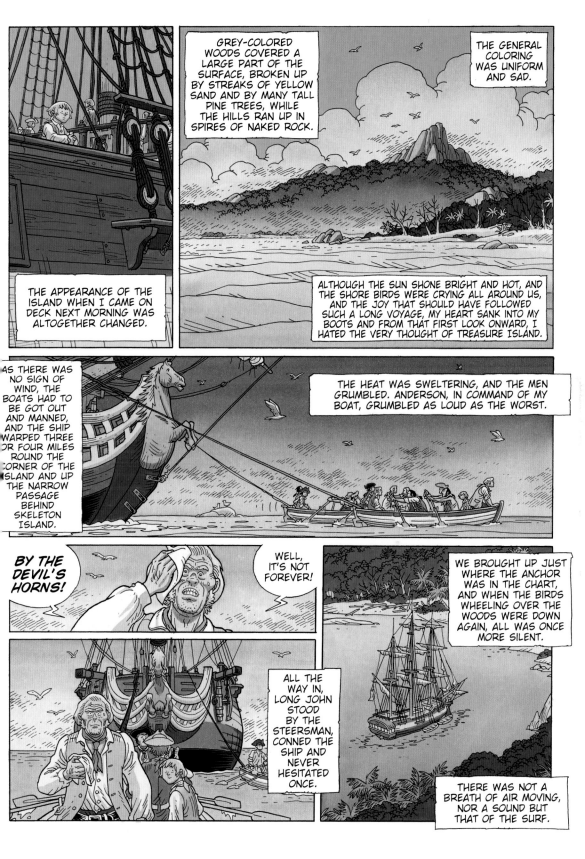

GREY-COLORED WOODS COVERED A LARGE PART OF THE SURFACE, BROKEN UP BY STREAKS OF YELLOW SAND AND BY MANY TALL PINE TREES, WHILE THE HILLS RAN UP IN SPIRES OF NAKED ROCK.

THE GENERAL COLORING WAS UNIFORM AND SAD.

THE APPEARANCE OF THE ISLAND WHEN I CAME ON DECK NEXT MORNING WAS ALTOGETHER CHANGED.

ALTHOUGH THE SUN SHONE BRIGHT AND HOT, AND THE SHORE BIRDS WERE CRYING ALL AROUND US, AND THE JOY THAT SHOULD HAVE FOLLOWED SUCH A LONG VOYAGE, MY HEART SANK INTO MY BOOTS AND FROM THAT FIRST LOOK ONWARD, I HATED THE VERY THOUGHT OF TREASURE ISLAND.

AS THERE WAS NO SIGN OF WIND, THE BOATS HAD TO BE GOT OUT AND MANNED, AND THE SHIP WARPED THREE OR FOUR MILES ROUND THE CORNER OF THE ISLAND AND UP THE NARROW PASSAGE BEHIND SKELETON ISLAND.

THE HEAT WAS SWELTERING, AND THE MEN GRUMBLED. ANDERSON, IN COMMAND OF MY BOAT, GRUMBLED AS LOUD AS THE WORST.

BY THE DEVIL'S HORNS!

WELL, IT'S NOT FOREVER!

WE BROUGHT UP JUST WHERE THE ANCHOR WAS IN THE CHART, AND WHEN THE BIRDS WHEELING OVER THE WOODS WERE DOWN AGAIN, ALL WAS ONCE MORE SILENT.

ALL THE WAY IN, LONG JOHN STOOD BY THE STEERSMAN, CONNED THE SHIP AND NEVER HESITATED ONCE.

THERE WAS NOT A BREATH OF AIR MOVING, NOR A SOUND BUT THAT OF THE SURF.

IF THE CONDUCT OF THE MEN HAD BEEN ALARMING IN THE BOATS, IT BECAME TRULY THREATENING WHEN THEY HAD COME ABOARD.

THEY LAY ABOUT THE DECK GROWLING TOGETHER IN TALK. THE SLIGHTEST ORDER WAS RECEIVED WITH A BLACK LOOK. MUTINY IT WAS PLAIN, HUNG OVER US LIKE A THUNDERCLOUD.

AND IT WAS NOT ONLY WE WHO PERCEIVED THE DANGER. LONG JOHN FAIRLY OUTSTRIPPED HIMSELF IN WILLINGNESS AND CIVILITY; HE WAS ALL SMILES TO EVERYONE. HE KEPT UP ONE SONG AFTER ANOTHER, AS IF TO CONCEAL THE DISCONTENT OF THE REST.

GENTLEMEN, WE'RE AT THE EDGE OF THE ABYSS.

NOW WE'VE ONLY ONE MAN TO RELY ON: SILVER. HE'S AS ANXIOUS AS YOU AND I TO SMOTHER THINGS UP.

LET'S ALLOW THE MEN AN AFTERNOON ASHORE. IF THEY ALL GO, THE SHIP WILL BE OURS.

LOADED PISTOLS WERE SERVED OUT TO ALL THE SURE MEN; HUNTER, JOYCE, AND REDRUTH RECEIVED THE NEWS WITH LESS SURPRISE THAN WE HAD LOOKED FOR.

MY LADS!

WE'VE HAD A HOT DAY AND ARE ALL TIRED AND OUT OF SORTS.

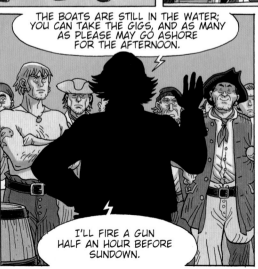

THE BOATS ARE STILL IN THE WATER; YOU CAN TAKE THE GIGS, AND AS MANY AS PLEASE MAY GO ASHORE FOR THE AFTERNOON.

I'LL FIRE A GUN HALF AN HOUR BEFORE SUNDOWN.

HURRAH!!

THE CAPTAIN WHIPPED OUT OF SIGHT IN A MOMENT, LEAVING SILVER TO ARRANGE THE PARTY.

AT LAST THE PARTY WAS MADE UP. SIX FELLOWS WERE TO STAY ON BOARD, AND THE REMAINING THIRTEEN, INCLUDING SILVER, BEGAN TO EMBARK.

IT WAS AS WELL HE DID SO, FOR IT WAS AS PLAIN AS DAY, SILVER WAS THE CAPTAIN OF A MIGHTY REBELLIOUS CREW.

IF SIX MEN WERE LEFT BY SILVER, IT WAS PLAIN OUR PARTY COULD NOT TAKE THE SHIP AND, CONSEQUENTLY, THEY HAD NO PRESENT NEED OF ME.

IT OCCURRED TO ME AT ONCE TO GO ASHORE.

JIM?!

IS THAT YOU, JIM?

YES, SIR, I WANTED TO COME ALONG WITH YOU, TOO.

MMM...

THE CREWS RACED FOR THE BEACH.

THE BOAT I WAS IN, HAVING SOME START AND THE BETTER MANNED, SHOT FAR AHEAD OF HER CONSORT.

JIM!!

JIM!

JUMPING, DUCKING, AND BREAKING THROUGH, I RAN STRAIGHT BEFORE MY NOSE, TILL I COULD RUN NO LONGER.

I WAS SO PLEASED AT HAVING GIVEN THE SLIP TO LONG JOHN THAT I BEGAN TO ENJOY MYSELF AND LOOK AROUND ME WITH SOME INTEREST.

I WAS UPON THE SKIRTS OF AN OPEN PIECE OF COUNTRY WITH ONE OF THE HILLS BEFORE ME.

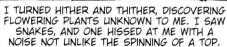

I TURNED HITHER AND THITHER, DISCOVERING FLOWERING PLANTS UNKNOWN TO ME. I SAW SNAKES, AND ONE HISSED AT ME WITH A NOISE NOT UNLIKE THE SPINNING OF A TOP.

THEN I CAME TO A LONG THICKET OF THESE OAK-LIKE TREES--LIVE OAKS, I HEARD AFTERWARD, WHICH STRETCHED DOWN TO A BROAD, REEDY FEN.

SUD-DENLY...

I JUDGED AT ONCE THAT SOME OF MY SHIP-MATES MUST BE DRAWING NEAR. NOR WAS I DECEIVED, FOR SOON I HEARD A DISTANT VOICE, WHICH GREW STEADILY LOUDER AND NEARER.

ANOTHER VOICE ANSWERED, AND THEN THE FIRST VOICE, WHICH I NOW RECOGNIZED TO BE SILVER'S. THEY MUST HAVE BEEN TALKING ALMOST FIERCELY, BUT NO DISTINCT WORD CAME TO MY HEARING.

CRAWLING ON ALL FOURS, I MADE STEADILY BUT SLOWLY TOWARDS THEM.

MATE, IF I HADN'T TOOK TO YOU LIKE PITCH, DO YOU THINK I'D HAVE BEEN HERE A-WARNING YOU?

IT'S TO SAVE YOUR NECK!

SILVER, YOU MEAN YOU'RE WITH THAT KIND OF A MESS OF SWABS?

NOT YOU!

AS FOR ME, IF I TURN AG'IN MY DOOTY--

VOOM

AAAAAAAARRH

JOHN!

HANDS OFF!

BUT, IN HEAVEN'S NAME, TELL ME WHAT WAS THAT?

THAT?

OH, I RECKON THAT'LL BE ALAN.

ALAN!

THEN REST HIS SOUL FOR A TRUE SEAMAN!

AND AS FOR YOU, LONG JOHN, YOU'VE BEEN A MATE OF MINE, BUT YOU'RE MATE OF MINE NO MORE.

KILL ME, TOO, IF YOU CAN. BUT I DEFIES YOU.

POK

AAH!!

FROM MY PLACE OF AMBUSH, I COULD HEAR SILVER PANT AS HE STRUCK THE BLOWS.

FOR A BRIEF MOMENT, EVERYTHING WAS LIKE A FOG BEFORE MY EYES.

WHEN I CAME AGAIN TO MYSELF, THE MONSTER HAD PULLED HIMSELF TOGETHER, HIS CRUTCH UNDER HIS ARM, HIS HAT UPON HIS HEAD.

JOHN PUT HIS HAND INTO HIS POCKET, BROUGHT OUT A WHISTLE, AND BLEW IT IN ORDER TO SUMMON HIS COMRADES, NO DOUBT.

I CRAWLED BACK AGAIN. AS SOON AS I WAS CLEAR OF THE THICKET, I RAN AS I NEVER RAN BEFORE.

AND AS I RAN, FEAR GREW UPON ME UNTIL IT TURNED INTO A KIND OF FRENZY.

INDEED, COULD ANYONE BE MORE ENTIRELY LOST THAN I?

IT WAS ALL OVER. THERE WAS NOTHING LEFT FOR ME BUT DEATH BY STARVATION OR BY THE HANDS OF THE MUTINEERS.

HOW COULD I REJOIN THOSE FIENDS, STILL BLOODIED FROM THEIR CRIME?

ALL THE WHILE, WITHOUT TAKING ANY NOTICE, I'D DRAWN NEAR TO THE FOOT OF THE HILL WITH THE TWO PEAKS.

HERE A FRESH ALARM BROUGHT ME TO A STANDSTILL WITH A THUMPING HEART.

WHAT IT WAS, BEAR OR MAN OR MONKEY, I COULD IN NO WISE TELL.

IT SEEMED DARK AND SHAGGY, AND THIS NEW APPARITION BROUGHT ME TO A STAND.

I TURNED ON MY HEEL, BUT THE FIGURE BEGAN TO HEAD ME OFF.

IT FLITTED LIKE A DEER, RUNNING MANLIKE ON TWO LEGS.

I STOOD STILL THEREFORE, AND CAST ABOUT FOR SOME METHOD OF ESCAPE.

WHILE I WAS EXPERIENCING STRANGE ADVENTURES ON THE ISLAND, THE DOCTOR, THE CAPTAIN, AND THE SQUIRE WERE SEEKING A MEANS TO SEIZE THE UPPER-HAND.

BUT THE WIND WAS WANTING, WHICH PREVENTED LEAVING WITH THE BOAT--

--WITHOUT TAKING INTO ACCOUNT THE SIX SCOUNDRELS GRUMBLING UNDER A SAIL IN THE FORECASTLE.

WAITING BEING A STRAIN, IT WAS DECIDED THAT HUNTER AND THE DOCTOR SHOULD GO ASHORE IN QUEST OF INFORMATION.

THE TWO MEN DIDN'T LAND AT THE SAME PLACE AS THE MUTINEERS, BUT A WAYS DOWN THE COAST.

THEY'D BEEN WALKING FOR SCARCELY TWO MINUTES WHEN THEY DISCOVERED THE STOCKADE.

A SPRING OF CLEAR WATER ROSE ALMOST AT THE TOP OF A KNOLL, AROUND WHICH THEY HAD CLAPPED A STOUT LOG HOUSE, LOOPHOLED FOR MUSKETRY, COMPLETED BY A PALING SIX FEET HIGH, WITHOUT DOOR OR OPENING.

THE PEOPLE IN THE LOG HOUSE HAD EVERY ADVANTAGE, FOR, SHORT OF A COMPLETE SURPRISE, THEY MIGHT HAVE HELD THE PLACE AGAINST A REGIMENT.

WHAT PARTICULARLY TOOK THE DOCTOR'S FANCY WAS THE SPRING, FOR IN THE CABIN OF THE HISPANIOLA, THEY HAD PLENTY OF ARMS AND AMMUNITION AND THINGS TO EAT, BUT NO WATER.

AAA... AAA... ARRH

DOCTOR LIVESEY, WHO HAD SERVED UNDER THE ORDERS OF THE DUKE OF CUMBERLAND, RECOGNIZED THE CRY OF A DYING MAN.

THEY LEAPT INTO THE LITTLE BOAT AND RAPIDLY RETURNED TO THE SCHOONER.

THE SQUIRE WAS SITTING DOWN, AS WHITE AS A SHEET.

AND ONE OF THE SIX FORECASTLE HANDS WAS LITTLE BETTER.

HE CAME NIGH-HAND FAINTING WHEN HE HEARD THE CRY.

ANOTHER TOUCH OF THE RUDDER AND THAT MAN WOULD JOIN US.

WHILE REDRUTH STOOD GUARD, HUNTER, JOYCE, AND THE DOCTOR LOADED THE BOAT WITH VARIOUS SUPPLIES AND MUNITIONS.

MR. HANDS!

HERE ARE TWO OF US WITH A BRACE OF PISTOLS EACH.

IF ANY OF YOU MAKES A SIGNAL OF ANY DESCRIPTION, THAT MAN'S DEAD.

THE MEN TRIED TO TAKE THEM FROM THE REAR BUT WHEN THEY SAW REDRUTH AND HIS MUSKETS, THEY BEAT A RETREAT AND KEPT QUIET.

THE BOAT WELL-LADEN, JOYCE, HUNTER, AND THE DOCTOR TOOK THEIR PLACES ON BOARD AND LEFT ON A SECOND TRIP.

AS FOR ME, I DECIDED TO WALK STRAIGHT TOWARDS THE MAN AND, AT THAT MOMENT, HE TOOK A STEP TO MEET ME.

HE WAS A BLUE-EYED WHITE MAN WITH SKIN SO BURNED EVEN HIS LIPS WERE BLACK, WEARING TATTERS OF OLD SHIP'S CANVAS AND OLD SEA CLOTH, HELD TOGETHER BY A SYSTEM OF THE MOST VARIOUS AND INCONGRUOUS FASTENINGS.

WHO ARE YOU?

BEN GUNN.

I'M POOR BEN GUNN, I AM, AND I HAVEN'T SPOKE WITH A CHRISTIAN THESE THREE YEARS.

THREE YEARS! WERE YOU SHIPWRECKED?

NAY, MATE MAROONED.

THE WORD STOOD FOR A PUNISHMENT COMMON ENOUGH AMONG THE BUCCANEERS, IN WHICH THE OFFENDER IS PUT ASHORE WITH A LITTLE POWDER AND SHOT.

I'VE LIVED ON GOATS, AND BERRIES, AND OYSTERS, BUT MY HEART IS SORE FOR CHRISTIAN DIET.

YOU MIGHTN'T HAPPEN TO HAVE A PIECE OF CHEESE ABOUT YOU, NOW?

IF EVER I CAN GET ABOARD AGAIN, YOU SHALL HAVE CHEESE.

WHAT DO YOU CALL YOURSELF, MATE?

JIM.

WELL NOW, JIM, I WAS A CIVIL, PIOUS BOY AND COULD RATTLE OFF MY CATECHISM THAT FAST.

AND HERE'S WHAT IT COME TO, JIM, AND IT BEGUN WITH CHUCK-FARTHEN ON THE GRAVESTONES!

MY MOTHER TOLD ME, SHE DID!

I'VE THOUGHT IT ALL OUT IN THIS HERE LONELY ISLAND AND I'M BACK ON PIETY. I'M BOUND I'LL BE GOOD--AND ALSO--

I'M RICH.

NOW, JIM, YOU TELL ME TRUE: THAT AIN'T FLINT'S SHIP?

NO, BUT IT'S SILVER'S.

I TOLD HIM THE WHOLE STORY OF OUR VOYAGE AND IN THE PREDICAMENT IN WHICH WE FOUND OURSELVES.

DO YOU THINK YOUR SQUIRE WOULD PROVE A LIBERAL-MINDED ONE IN CASE OF HELP.

I'M CERTAIN OF IT.

I'LL TELL YOU WHAT AND NO MORE. I WERE IN FLINT'S SHIP WHEN HE BURIED THE TREASURE; HE AND SIX STRONG SEAMEN.

WE WERE WAITING FOR HIM IN THE OLD *WALRUS*, AND HE CAME BACK, BUT NOT THE SIX OTHERS.

WELL, I WAS IN ANOTHER SHIP THREE YEARS BACK, AND WE SIGHTED THIS ISLAND. 'BOYS,' SAID I, 'HERE'S FLINT'S TREASURE.' TWELVE DAYS WE LOOKED FOR IT, BUT IN VAIN.

UNTIL ONE FINE MORNING ALL HANDS WENT ABOARD, LEAVING ME HERE.

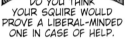

DON'T UNDERSTAND ONE WORD THAT YOU'VE BEEN SAYING. BUT THAT'S NEITHER HERE NOR THERE, FOR HOW AM I TO GET ON BOARD?

I MADE A BOAT, WE COULD—

BRAOOOMM

THEY HAVE BEGUN TO FIGHT!

LEFT! KEEP TO YOUR LEFT HAND, MATE! UNDER THE TREES WITH YOU! THAT'S WHERE I KILLED MY FIRST GOAT!

FARTHER OFF, DOCTOR LIVESEY'S SECOND TRIP FAIRLY AROUSED THE WATCHERS THAT SILVER HAD POSTED ON THE BEACH TO KEEP AN EYE ON THE BOATS.

ONCE THEY'D REACHED SHORE, THE THREE MEN SET TO RESUPPLYING THE BLOCKHOUSE.

LEAVING JOYCE WITH HALF A DOZEN MUSKETS TO GUARD THEM, THEY RETURNED TO THE BOAT AND LOADED ONCE MORE.

SO THEY PROCEEDED TILL THE WHOLE CARGO WAS BESTOWED.

THE TWO SERVANTS TOOK THEIR POSITIONS IN THE BLOCKHOUSE, AND THE DOCTOR, WITH ALL HIS POWER, SCULLED BACK TO THE HISPANIOLA.

THE SQUIRE, ALL HIS FAINTNESS GONE FROM HIM, WAS WAITING TO HELP THE DOCTOR MAKE FAST THE BOAT, THEN TO LOAD IT AGAIN, WITH PORK, POWDER, AND BISCUIT, AS WELL AS A MUSKET AND A CUTLASS FOR EACH OF THEM.

THE REST OF THE ARMS AND POWDER WERE DROPPED OVERBOARD, WHILE REDRUTH REJOINED THEM ON BOARD THE BOAT.

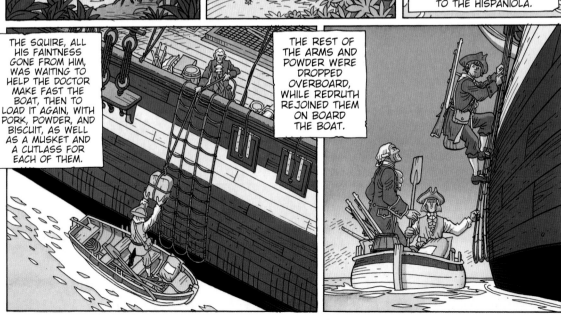

THEY THEN BROUGHT THE BOAT ROUND TO THE SHIP'S COUNTER, TO BE HANDIER FOR CAPTAIN SMOLLETT.

PANIOLA

NOW, MEN, DO YOU HEAR ME?

ABRAHAM GRAY--IT'S TO YOU I AM SPEAKING. I AM LEAVING THIS SHIP AND I ORDER YOU TO FOLLOW YOUR CAPTAIN.

I KNOW YOU ARE A GOOD MAN.

AND I DARESAY NOT ONE OF YOU'S AS BAD AS HE MAKES OUT. I GIVE YOU THIRTY SECONDS.

COME, DON'T HANG SO LONG IN STAYS.

THERE WAS A SUDDEN SCUFFLE, A SOUND OF BLOWS, AND THEN--

BLING

I'M WITH YOU, SIR!

AND THE NEXT MOMENT, THEY HAD DROPPED ABOARD OF US, AND THEY HAD SHOVED OFF.

THE FIFTH TRIP WAS QUITE DIFFERENT FROM ANY OF THE OTHERS.

WITH FIVE MEN AND THE SUPPLIES, THE LITTLE BOAR WAS GRAVELY OVERLOADED.

AND A STRONG RIPPLING CURRENT WAS SWEEPING IT WESTWARD, TOWARDS THE SAME SPOT WHERE SILVER AND THE OTHERS HAD GONE ASHORE.

I CANNOT KEEP HER HEAD FOR THE STOCK-ADE, SIR.

YOU MUST BEAR UP UNTIL YOU SEE YOU'RE GAINING.

WE'LL NEVER GET ASHORE AT THIS RATE.

IT'S THE ONLY COURSE WE CAN LIE.

WE MUST...*OH!*

THE FIVE ROGUES STILL ON BOARD WERE BUSY ABOUT THE LONG NINE.

THE GUN!

ISRAEL WAS FLINT'S GUNNER.

WHO'S THE BEST SHOT?

MR. TRELAWNEY, OUT AND AWAY.

MR. TRELAWNEY, WILL YOU PLEASE PICK ME OFF ONE OF THOSE MEN, SIR? HANDS, IF POSSIBLE--

THE SQUIRE RAISED HIS GUN, AND THE ROWING CEASED.

HOWEVER, THEY HAD NO LUCK.

HANDS WASN'T HIT.

AAAH!

THE CRY HE GAVE WAS ECHOED, NOT ONLY BY HIS COMPANIONS ON BOARD, BUT FROM THE OTHER PIRATES TROOPING OUT ON SHORE AND TUMBLING INTO THEIR PLACES IN THE BOATS.

IF WE CAN'T GET ASHORE, ALL'S UP.

THE BOAT WAS NOW NEAR A NARROW SANDBAR, WHEN--

WATCH OUT!

BRAOOOOM

THE BALL PASSED OVER THE BOAT, BUT THE LATTER SANK BY THE STERN, LEAVING THE PASSENGERS FLOUNDERING IN THE WATER.

THEY WERE SAFE AND SOUND, BUT ALL THEIR STORES WERE AT THE BOTTOM, AND ONLY TWO GUNS REMAINED IN A STATE OF SERVICE.

THAT'S WHEN THEY HEARD VOICES DRAWING NEAR THEM ALONGSHORE.

THIS WAY!! QUICK!

HURRY, BEFORE THEY CUT US OFF FROM THE PATH TO THE STOCKADE!

THEY'RE GETTING CLOSE!

GRAY, YOU DON'T HAVE ANY WEAPONS?

HERE!

THANKS.

YYAAAAAHH!!!

LET'S GO SEE WHICH WRETCH MET HIS DEATH.

AAH!

BLAM BLAM

TO THE STOCKADE! QUICK!

THIS RETURN VOLLEY HAD SCATTERED THE MUTINEERS, WHICH ALLOWED THEM TO TRANSPORT POOR REDRUTH INTO THE LOG HOUSE.

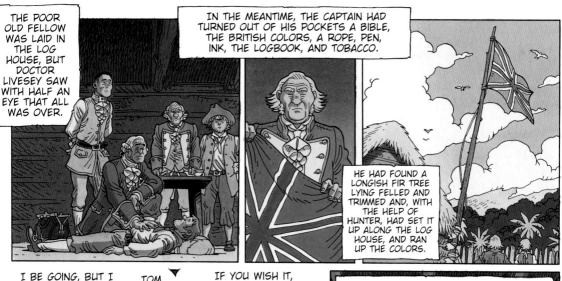

THE POOR OLD FELLOW WAS LAID IN THE LOG HOUSE, BUT DOCTOR LIVESEY SAW WITH HALF AN EYE THAT ALL WAS OVER.

IN THE MEANTIME, THE CAPTAIN HAD TURNED OUT OF HIS POCKETS A BIBLE, THE BRITISH COLORS, A ROPE, PEN, INK, THE LOGBOOK, AND TOBACCO.

HE HAD FOUND A LONGISH FIR TREE LYING FELLED AND TRIMMED AND, WITH THE HELP OF HUNTER, HAD SET IT UP ALONG THE LOG HOUSE, AND RAN UP THE COLORS.

I BE GOING, BUT I WISH I HAD A LICK AT THEM WITH THE GUN FIRST.

TOM, SAY YOU FORGIVE ME.

IF YOU WISH IT, SO BE IT, AMEN!

COULD SOMEBODY READ A PRAYER?

IT'S THE CUSTOM, SIR.

AND NOT LONG AFTER, WITHOUT ANOTHER WORD, HE PASSED AWAY.

DON'T YOU TAKE ON, SIR. NO FEAR FOR A MAN WHO'S FALLEN DOING HIS DUTY.

IT'S OUR OWN SALVATION THAT WORRIES ME.

HOW DO YOU MEAN?

IT'S A PITY, SIR, THAT WE LOST THAT SECOND LOAD. AS FOR POWDER AND SHOT, WE'LL DO. BUT THE RATIONS ARE SHORT, VERY SHORT.

BRACOUMMM

NOW, THERE'S YOUR FRIENDS, SURE ENOUGH.

FAR MORE LIKELY IT'S THE MUTINEERS.

THAT! SILVER WOULD FLY THE JOLLY ROGER! NO, THAT'S YOUR FRIENDS IN THE OLD STOCKADE MADE BY FLINT! AH, THAT FLINT HE WAS AFRAID OF NONE, NOT HE, SAVE SILVER.

WELL, ALL THE MORE REASON I SHOULD HURRY ON AND JOIN MY FRIENDS.

YOU'RE A GOOD BOY, OR I'M MISTOOK.

NOW, BEN GUNN'S A CLEVER ONE.

AND WHEN BEN GUNN IS WANTED, YOU KNOW WHERE TO FIND HIM, JIM. AND HIM THAT COMES IS TO HAVE A WHITE THING IN HIS HAND AND HE'S TO COME ALONE. AND WHEN? SAYS YOU. WHY FROM ABOUT NOON OBSERVATION TO ABOUT SIX BELLS.

I RECKON YOU CAN GO, JIM. IF YOU WAS TO SEE SILVER, YOU WOULDN'T GO FOR TO SELL BEN GUNN? WILD HORSES WOULDN'T DRAW IT FROM YOU? NO, SAYS YOU.

A CANNON BALL LANDED NOT A HUNDRED YARDS FROM WHERE WE TWO WERE TALKING.

THE NEXT MOMENT EACH OF US HAD TAKEN TO HIS HEELS IN A DIFFERENT DIRECTION.

WITH A ROAR AND A WHISTLE, A ROUND SHOT PASSED HIGH ABOVE THE ROOF OF THE LOG HOUSE.

OHO! BLAZE AWAY! YOU'VE LITTLE ENOUGH POWDER ALREADY, MY LADS.

THE SECOND BALL DESCENDED INSIDE THE STOCKADE, SCATTERING A CLOUD OF SAND.

IT MUST BE THE FLAG THEY ARE AIMING AT. WOULD IT NOT BE WISER TO TAKE IT IN?

STRIKE MY COLORS! NO, SIR, NOT I.

THERE IS ONE GOOD THING ABOUT ALL THIS. THE WOOD IN FRONT OF US IS LIKELY CLEAR AND, WITH THE LOW TIDE, OUR STORES SHOULD BE UNCOVERED.

ALL THROUGH THE EVENING THEY KEPT THUNDERING AWAY. BALL AFTER BALL FLEW OVER OR FELL SHORT, THOUGH ONE POPPED THROUGH THE ROOF AND FLOOR.

GRAY AND HUNTER WERE THE FIRST TO COME FORWARD, BUT IT PROVED A USELESS MISSION. THE MUTINEERS WERE BUSY LOADING OUR STORES ON A BOAT. SILVER WAS IN THE STERN SHEETS IN COMMAND.

THE CAPTAIN SAT DOWN TO HIS LOG--

FOR A GOOD HOUR, I MOVED FROM HIDING PLACE TO HIDING PLACE, ALWAYS PURSUED, OR SO IT SEEMED TO ME, BY THOSE TERRIFYING MISSILES.

AFTER A LONG DETOUR TO THE EAST, I CREPT DOWN AMONG THE SHORESIDE TREES.

THE SUN HAD JUST SET, THE TIDE WAS FAR OUT, AND THE AIR CHILLED ME THROUGH MY JACKET.

THE *HISPANIOLA* STILL LAY ANCHORED, BUT THERE WAS THE JOLLY ROGER--THE BLACK FLAG OF PIRACY--FLYING FROM HER PEAK.

BRACOOOUM

THERE CAME ANOTHER RED FLASH AND, THE LAST OF THE CANNONADE WHISTLED THROUGH THE AIR.

MEN WERE DEMOLISHING SOMETHING WITH AXES ON THE BEACH; THE POOR JOLLY BOAT, I AFTERWARD DISCOVERED.

AWAY, NEAR THE MOUTH OF THE RIVER, A GREAT FIRE WAS GLOWING WHILE A GIG KEPT COMING AND GOING AND THE MEN WERE SINGING, BUT WITH A SOUND IN THEIR VOICES WHICH SUGGESTED RUM.

SKIRTING THE WOODS, I REGAINED THE REAR OF THE STOCKADE.

DOCTOR? HELLO!

CAPTAIN! SQUIRE! SOMEONE'S HAILING US!

CAPTAIN? HUNTER, IS THAT YOU?

JIM?!

JIM!!

DOCTOR!!

HA HA HA!

I HAD SOON TOLD MY STORY AND BEGAN TO LOOK ABOUT ME.

THE LOG HOUSE WAS MADE OF UNSQUARED TRUNKS OF PINE.

THERE WAS AN ARTIFICIAL BASIN MADE OF A KETTLE AND SUNK INTO THE SAND.

IN THE CENTER, A STONE SLAB LAID DOWN BY WAY OF HEARTH, AND AN OLD RUSTY IRON BASKET FOR THE FIRE.

THE EVENING BREEZE WHISTLED THROUGH EVERY CHINK, LETTING IN A RAIN OF FINE SAND. THERE WAS SAND IN OUR WATER, OUR FOOD, EVEN OUR EYES AND MOUTHS.

IT WAS BUT A LITTLE PART OF THE SMOKE THAT FOUND ITS WAY OUT, AND THE REST EDDIED ABOUT THE HOUSE AND KEPT US COUGHING.

IF WE HAD BEEN ALLOWED TO SIT IDLE WE SHOULD ALL HAVE FALLEN IN THE BLUES.

BUT CAPTAIN SMOLLETT CALLED US UP AND DIVIDED US INTO WATCHES.

TWO WERE SENT OUT FOR FIREWOOD; TWO MORE WERE SET TO DIG A GRAVE FOR REDRUTH; THE DOCTOR WAS NAMED COOK; I WAS PUT SENTRY AT THE DOOR.

SMOLLETT IS A BETTER MAN THAN I AM.

AND THAT MEANS A GOOD DEAL, JIM. AS FOR THAT BEN GUNN--

HE'S HALF CRAZY.

ONE WOULD EXPECT SO, JIM.

WAS IT CHEESE. YOU SAID HE HAD A FANCY FOR?

YES, SIR, CHEESE.

DID YOU KNOW MY SNUFFBOX CARRIES A PIECE OF PARMESAN CHEESE?

WELL, THAT'S FOR BEN GUNN!

BEFORE SUPPER WAS EATEN WE BURIED OLD TOM IN THE SAND AND STOOD ROUND HIM FOR A WHILE.

WHEN WE HAD EATEN OUR PORK AND HAD A STIFF GLASS OF GROG, THE THREE CHIEFS GOT TOGETHER IN A CORNER.

FROM NINETEEN, THE MUTINEERS WERE ALREADY REDUCED TO FIFTEEN, TWO OTHERS WOUNDED, BUT OUR BEST HOPE WAS TO KILL OFF THE BUCCANEERS UNTIL THEY EITHER HAULED DOWN THEIR FLAG OR RAN AWAY WITH THE HISPANIOLA.

I SLEPT LIKE A LOG OF WOOD. THE REST HAD ALREADY BREAKFASTED AND INCREASED THE PILE OF FIREWOOD BY ABOUT HALF, WHEN I WAS AWAKENED BY THE SOUNDS OF VOICES.

FLAG OF TRUCE!

SILVER HIMSELF!

THERE WERE TWO MEN JUST OUTSIDE THE STOCKADE.

ONE OF THEM WAS WAVING A WHITE CLOTH; THE OTHER, SILVER HIMSELF, STANDING PLACIDLY BY.

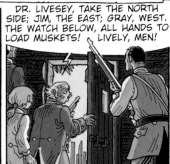

THEY WADED KNEE-DEEP IN A LOW WHITE VAPOR CRAWLED OUT OF THE MORASS, WHICH TOLD A POOR TALE OF THE HEALTHINESS OF THE ISLAND.

KEEP INDOORS, MEN. TEN TO ONE, THIS IS A TRICK.

WHO GOES? STAND, OR WE FIRE!

FLAG OF TRUCE!

DR. LIVESEY, TAKE THE NORTH SIDE; JIM, THE EAST; GRAY, WEST. THE WATCH BELOW, ALL HANDS TO LOAD MUSKETS! LIVELY, MEN!

AND WHAT DO YOU WANT WITH YOUR FLAG OF TRUCE?

CAP'N SILVER, SIR, TO COME ON BOARD AND MAKE TERMS.

CAP'N SILVER! WHO'S HE?

ME, SIR.

THESE POOR LADS HAVE CHOSEN ME CAP'N AFTER YOUR DESERTION, SIR.

WE'RE WILLING TO SUBMIT, IF WE CAN COME TO TERMS.

ALL I ASK IS YOUR WORD TO LET ME SAFE AND SOUND OUT OF THIS HERE STOCKADE.

IF YOU WISH TO TALK TO ME, YOU CAN COME, THAT'S ALL.

IF THERE'S ANY TREACHERY, IT'LL BE ON YOUR SIDE, AND THE LORD HELP YOU.

THAT'S ENOUGH, CAP'N.

SILVER THREW HIS CRUTCH OVER THE PALISADE BEFORE SURMOUNTING IT AND DROPPING SAFELY TO THE OTHER SIDE.

SILVER HAD TERRIBLE HARD WORK GETTING UP THE KNOLL.

I WAS FAR TOO TAKEN UP WITH THIS TO BE OF THE SLIGHTEST USE AS SENTRY; INDEED, I'D ALREADY DESERTED MY LOOPHOLE AND CREPT UP BEHIND THE CAPTAIN.

BUT HE STUCK TO IT LIKE A MAN IN SILENCE AND AT LAST ARRIVED BEFORE THE CAPTAIN, WHOM HE SALUTED IN THE HANDSOMEST STYLE.

HERE YOU ARE, MY MAN. YOU'D BETTER SIT DOWN.

YOU AIN'T A-GOING TO LET ME INSIDE, CAP'N? WITH THIS COLD?

IF YOU'D PLEASED TO BE AN HONEST MAN, YOU MIGHT HAVE BEEN SITTING IN YOUR GALLEY. YOU'RE EITHER MY SHIP'S COOK OR A COMMON PIRATE, AND THEN YOU CAN GO HANG!

WELL, WELL, CAP'N.

AH, THERE'S JIM!

'TOP OF THE MORNING, JIM! DOCTOR, MY RESPECTS.

WELL, THAT WAS A GOOD LAY OF YOURS LAST NIGHT. I DON'T DENY IT. AND I'LL NOT DENY NEITHER BUT WHAT SOME OF MY PEOPLE WAS SHOOK, THAT'S WHY I'M HERE FOR TERMS.

BUT YOU MARK ME, CAP'N, IT WON'T DO TWICE. WE'LL HAVE TO DO SENTRY-GO!

ALL THAT SILVER SAID WAS AN ENIGMA TO THE CAPTAIN, BUT I BEGAN TO SUPPOSE THAT BEN GUNN HAD PAID THE BUCCANEERS A VISIT WHILE THEY ALL LAY DRUNK ROUND THEIR FIRE.

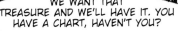

THAT'S AS MAY BE.

WHAT I MEAN IS, WE WANT YOUR CHART. NOW, I NEVER MEANT YOU NO HARM, MYSELF.

WE WANT THAT TREASURE AND WE'LL HAVE IT. YOU HAVE A CHART, HAVEN'T YOU?

THAT WON'T DO WITH ME, MY MAN. WE KNOW EXACTLY WHAT YOU MEANT TO DO AND WE DON'T CARE, FOR NOW YOU CAN'T DO IT.

SEEIN' AS HOW YOU ARE ABOUT TO TAKE A PIPE, CAP'N, I'LL MAKE SO FREE AS TO DO LIKEWISE.

NOW, YOU GIVE US THE CHART TO GET THE TREASURE BY AND DROP STOVING IN THE HEADS OF POOR SEAMEN WHILE ASLEEP.

YOU DO THAT, AND WE'LL OFFER YOU A CHOICE. EITHER YOU COME ABOARD ALONG WITH US AND THEN I'LL GIVE YOU MY AFFY-DAVY TO CLAP YOU SOMEWHERE SAFE ASHORE, OR YOU CAN STAY HERE.

WE'LL DIVIDE STORES WITH YOU, AND I'LL GIVE YOU MY AFFY-DAVY TO SPEAK THE FIRST SHIP I SIGHT.

AND I HOPE THAT HANDS IN THIS HERE BLOCKHOUSE WILL OVERHAUL MY WORDS, FOR WHAT IS SPOKE TO ONE IS SPOKE TO ALL.

IS THAT ALL?

EVERY LAST WORD, BY THUNDER! REFUSE THAT AND YOU'VE SEEN THE LAST OF ME BUT MUSKET BALLS!

VERY GOOD. NOW YOU'LL HEAR ME.

IF YOU'LL COME UP ONE BY ONE, UNARMED, I'LL ENGAGE TO CLAP YOU ALL IN IRONS, AND TAKE YOU HOME TO A FAIR TRIAL IN ENGLAND.

IF YOU WON'T, I'LL SEE YOU ALL TO DAVY JONES.

YOU CAN'T FIND THE TREASURE. YOU CAN'T SAIL THE SHIP--THERE'S NOT A MAN AMONG YOU FIT TO SAIL THE SHIP. YOU CAN'T FIGHT US.

I STAND HERE AND TELL YOU SO, AND THEY'RE THE LAST GOOD WORDS YOU'LL GET FROM ME.

AND NOW BUNDLE OUT, FOR I SWEAR TO YOU THAT I'LL PUT A BULLET IN YOUR BACK WHEN NEXT I MEET YOU.

SILVER'S EYES STARTED IN HIS HEAD WITH WRATH.

GIVE ME A HAND UP!

AS NOT A MAN MOVED, SILVER CRAWLED ALONG THE SAND--

TILL HE GOT HOLD OF THE WALL AND COULD HOIST HIMSELF AGAIN UPON HIS CRUTCH.

PFFT

THERE! THAT'S WHAT I THINK OF YE!

BEFORE AN HOUR'S OUT, I'LL STOVE IN YOUR OLD BLOCKHOUSE LIKE A RUM PUNCHEON! LAUGH, BY THUNDER! YE'LL SOON LAUGH UPON THE OTHER SIDE.

THEM THAT DIE'LL BE THE LUCKY ONES!

AND WITH A DREADFUL OATH HE STUMBLED OFF.

HE WAS HELPED ACROSS THE STOCKADE, AFTER FOUR OR FIVE FAILURES, BY THE MAN WITH THE FLAG OF TRUCE AND DISAPPEARED AMONG THE TREES.

AS SOON AS SILVER DISAPPEARED, THE CAPTAIN TURNED AND FOUND NOT A MAN OF US AT HIS POST BUT GRAY.

MR. TRELAWNEY, I'M SURPRISED AT YOU, SIR! DOCTOR, I THOUGHT YOU HAD WORN THE KING'S COAT!

EVERYONE HAD A RED FACE.

MY LADS, I'VE PITCHED IT IN RED-HOT ON PURPOSE WITH SILVER AND, BEFORE THE HOUR'S OUT, WE SHALL BE BOARDED. WE'RE OUTNUMBERED, BUT WE FIGHT IN SHELTER.

I'VE NO MANNER OF DOUBT THAT WE CAN DRUB THEM, IF YOU CHOOSE.

HAWKINS, HELP YOURSELF TO BREAKFAST AND BACK TO YOUR POST TO EAT IT.

ON THE EAST AND WEST, THERE WERE ONLY TWO LOOPHOLES, ON THE SOUTH SIDE, TWO AGAIN, AND ON THE NORTH SIDE, FIVE.

THERE WAS A ROUND SCORE OF MUSKETS FOR THE SEVEN OF US, WITH MUNITIONS LAID READY ON PILES OF FIREWOOD THAT SERVED US AS TABLES. IN THE MIDDLE, THE CUTLASSES LAY RANGED.

DOCTOR, YOU'LL TAKE THE DOOR.

HUNTER, TAKE THE EAST SIDE.

JOYCE, YOU STAND BY THE WEST.

MR. TRELAWNEY, YOU ARE THE BEST SHOT--YOU AND GRAY WILL THE FIVE LOOPHOLES ON THE NORTH SIDE.

HAWKINS, NEITHER YOU NOR I ARE MUCH ACCOUNT AT SHOOTING; WE'LL STAND BY TO LOAD AND BEAR A HAND.

AS SOON AS THE SUN HAD FALLEN UPON OUR CLEARING, THE SAND WAS BAKING, AND THE RESIN MELTING IN THE LOGS.

EACH ONE STOOD AT HIS POST, IN A FEVER OF HEAT AND ANXIETY.

AN HOUR PASSED AWAY.

NOTHING HAPPENED, BUT WE WERE ALL ON THE ALERT, MUSKETS IN HAND, THE CAPTAIN OUT IN THE MIDDLE OF THE BLOCKHOUSE, WITH HIS MOUTH VERY TIGHT AND A FROWN ON HIS FACE.

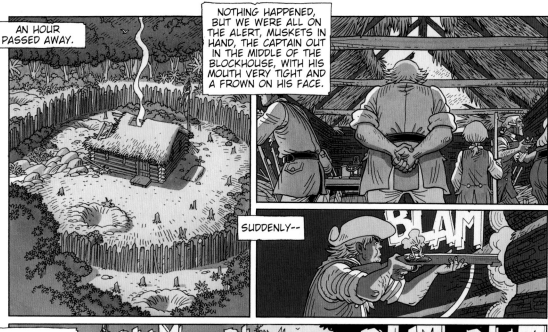

SUDDENLY--

BLAM

THE REPORT WAS REPEATED IN A SCATTERING VOLLEY FROM EVERY SIDE OF THE ENCLOSURE.

AM BLAM BLAM BLAM BLAM BLAM

AS THE SMOKE CLEARED AWAY, THE STOCKADE AND WOODS AROUND IT LOOKED AS QUIET AND EMPTY AS BEFORE.

DID YOU HIT YOUR MAN?

NO, SIR.

NEXT BEST THING TO TELL THE TRUTH.

HOW MANY SHOULD YOU SAY THERE WERE ON YOUR SIDE, DOCTOR? AND ON YOURS, MR. TRELAWNEY?

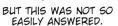

BUT THIS WAS NOT SO EASILY ANSWERED.

IT WAS PLAIN THAT THE ATTACK HAD COME FROM THE NORTH, BUT CAPTAIN SMOLLETT MADE NO CHANGE IN HIS ARRANGEMENTS.

NOR HAD WE MUCH TIME LEFT TO US FOR THOUGHT, FOR SUDDENLY--

BLAM BLAM BLAM

AT THE SAME MOMENT, THE FIRE WAS ONCE MORE OPENED FROM THE WOODS.

BLAM BLAM

PAK

AH!

BLAM

FOUR HAD MADE GOOD THEIR FOOTING INSIDE OUR DEFENSES, WHILE FROM THE SHELTER OF THE WOODS SEVEN OR EIGHT MEN KEPT UP A HOT THOUGH USELESS FIRE ON THE LOG HOUSE.

BLAM BLAM

AT 'EM, ALL HANDS-- ALL HANDSS--!!

SUDDENLY A PIRATE GRASPED HUNTER'S MUSKET AND WRENCHED IT.

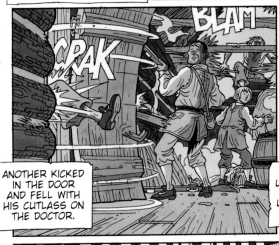

OUT, LADS, OUT!

ANOTHER KICKED IN THE DOOR AND FELL WITH HIS CUTLASS ON THE DOCTOR.

WE WERE FIGHTING UNDER COVER AND NOW IT WAS WE WHO LAY UNCOVERED AND COULD NOT RETURN A BLOW.

SNATCHING A KNIFE, I DASHED OUT OF THE DOOR--

AND FOUND MYSELF FACE TO FACE WITH ANDERSON.

CRIES AND CONFUSION, THE FLASHES AND REPORTS AND ONE LOUD GROAN RANG IN MY EARS.

?!

AAH!!

WHEN I FOUND MY FEET AGAIN, I SAW THAT GRAY HAD CUT DOWN THE BIG BOATSWAIN.

ANOTHER NOW LAY IN AGONY, THE PISTOL STILL SMOKING IN HIS HAND.

A THIRD, THE DOCTOR HAD DISPOSED OF AT A BLOW.

AND THE FOURTH TO HAVE SCALED THE PALISADE WAS NOW CLAMBERING OUT AGAIN.

IN THREE SECONDS NOTHING REMAINED OF THE ATTACKING PARTY BUT THE FIVE WHO HAD FALLEN, FOUR ON THE INSIDE AND ONE ON THE OUTSIDE OF THE PALISADE.

THE DOCTOR AND GRAY AND I RAN FULL SPEED FOR SHELTER BEFORE THE FIRE COULD RECOMMENCE.

THE SMOKE HAVING CLEARED SOMEWHAT, WE SAW THE PRICE WE HAD PAID FOR VICTORY.

HUNTER LAY BESIDE HIS LOOPHOLE, STUNNED.

JOYCE BY HIS, SHOT THROUGH THE HEAD.

RIGHT IN THE CENTER, THE SQUIRE WAS SUPPORTING THE CAPTAIN, ONE AS PALE AS THE OTHER.

HAVE THEY RUN?

ALL THAT COULD, YOU MAY BE BOUND!

BUT THERE'S FIVE OF THEM WILL NEVER RUN AGAIN.

FIVE! FIVE AGAINST THREE LEAVES US FOUR TO NINE. THAT'S BETTER ODDS THAN WE HAD AT STARTING.

THERE WAS NO RETURN OF THE MUTINEERS. THEY HAD "GOT THEIR RATIONS FOR THAT DAY," AS THE CAPTAIN PUT IT.

WE HAD QUIET TIME TO OVER-HAUL THE WOUNDED AND GET DINNER.

THE SQUIRE AND I COOKED OUTSIDE, FOR THE HORROR OF THE LOUD GROANS THAT REACHED US FROM THE DOCTOR'S PATIENTS.

ONLY THREE OUT OF THE EIGHT MEN WHO HAD FALLEN IN THE ACTION STILL BREATHED: ONE OF THE PIRATES, HUNTER, AND CAPTAIN SMOLLETT.

THE MUTINEER DIED UNDER THE DOCTOR'S KNIFE.

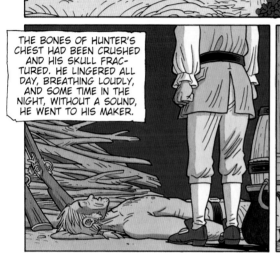

THE BONES OF HUNTER'S CHEST HAD BEEN CRUSHED AND HIS SKULL FRACTURED. HE LINGERED ALL DAY, BREATHING LOUDLY, AND SOME TIME IN THE NIGHT, WITHOUT A SOUND, HE WENT TO HIS MAKER.

AS FOR THE CAPTAIN, HIS WOUNDS WERE GRIEVOUS, BUT NOT DANGEROUS.

A BALL HAD BROKEN HIS SHOULDER BLADE AND TOUCHED HIS LUNG.

THE SECOND HAD ONLY TORN SOME MUSCLES IN HIS CALF.

HE WAS SURE TO RECOVER, BUT FOR WEEKS TO COME, HE MUST NOT WALK NOR MOVE HIS ARM, NOR SO MUCH AS SPEAK.

ONCE DONE TALKING, THE DOCTOR TOOK UP HIS HAT AND PISTOLS, GIRT ON A CUTLASS, PUT THE CHART IN HIS POCKET, AND WITH A MUSKET ON HIS SHOULDER CROSSED THE NORTHERN PALISADE AND QUICKLY DISAPPEARED FROM SIGHT.

WHY, IN THE NAME OF DAVY JONES, IS DR. LIVESEY MAD?

HE'S ABOUT THE LAST OF THIS CREW FOR THAT.

I TAKE IT THE DOCTOR HAS HIS IDEA AND, IF I'M RIGHT. HE'S GOING NOW TO SEE BEN GUNN.

I WAS RIGHT, AS APPEARED LATER, BUT IN THE MEANTIME, IT WAS STIFLING HOT AND THE SAND WAS ABLAZE WITH MIDDAY SUN.

I BEGAN TO GET ANOTHER THOUGHT INTO MY HEAD, WHICH WAS NOT BY ANY MEANS SO RIGHT.

I ENVIED THE DOCTOR, WALKING IN THE COOL SHADOW OF THE WOODS, WITH THE BIRDS ABOUT HIM, AND THE SMELL OF PINES.

WITH SO MUCH BLOOD AND SO MANY DEAD BODIES ABOUT ME, I TOOK A DISGUST OF THE PLACE ALMOST AS STRONG AS FEAR.

ALL THE TIME I WAS WASHING OUT THE BLOCKHOUSE AND THEN WASHING UP FROM DIN-NER, THIS FEELING KEPT GROWING STRONGER.

WITH NO ONE THEN OBSERVING ME, I FILLED BOTH POCKETS WITH BISCUIT.

I WAS A FOOL, IF YOU LIKE, BUT I WAS DETERMINED TO DO IT WITH ALL THE PRE-CAUTIONS IN MY POWER.

THE NEXT THING I LAID HOLD OF WAS A BRACE OF PISTOLS, TO COMPLETE THE POWDER HORN AND BULLETS I ALREADY HAD.

MY SCHEME WAS TO GO DOWN THE SANDY SPIT THAT DIVIDES THE ANCHORAGE FROM THE OPEN SEA AND ASCERTAIN WHETHER IT WAS THERE OR NOT THAT BEN GUNN HAD HIDDEN HIS BOAT.

THE SQUIRE AND GRAY WERE BUSY HELPING THE CAPTAIN WITH HIS BANDAGES, I MADE A BOLT FOR IT OVER THE STOCKADE AND INTO THE THICKEST OF THE TREES.

IT WAS ALREADY LATE IN THE AFTERNOON AND, WHILE WALKING, I COULD HEAR NOT ONLY THE THUNDER OF THE SURF, BUT A TOSSING OF FOLIAGE AND GRINDING OF BOUGHS, WHICH SHOWED ME THAT A STRONG WIND HAD SET IN.

I WALKED ALONG BESIDE THE SURF WITH GREAT ENJOYMENT TILL I TOOK THE COVER OF SOME THICK BUSHES AND CREPT UP TO THE RIDGE OF THE SPIT.

THE SEA BREEZE WAS ALREADY AT AN END, AND THE ANCHORAGE LAY STILL AND LEADEN AS WHEN FIRST WE ENTERED IT.

THE *HISPANIOLA* WAS REFLECTED FROM THE TRUNK TO THE WATERLINE, THE JOLLY ROGER HANGING FROM HER PEAK.

ALONGSIDE, I SPIED SILVER IN A GIG, APPARENTLY JOKING WITH TWO MEN LEANING OVER THE STERN BULWARKS.

ALL AT ONCE THERE BEGAN THE MOST HORRID SCREECHING, WHICH STARTLED ME BADLY, THOUGH I SOON REMEMBERED THE VOICE OF CAPTAIN FLINT.

I EVEN THOUGHT I COULD MAKE OUT THE BIRD, PERCHED UPON HER MASTER'S WRIST.

SHORTLY AFTER, THE BOAT SHOVED OFF, WHILE THE TWO MEN WENT BELOW BY THE CABIN COMPANION.

THE SUN HAD GONE DOWN BEHIND THE SPYGLASS, AND AS THE FOG WAS COLLECTING, IT BEGAN TO GROW DARK IN EARNEST.

THE WHITE ROCK, VISIBLE ABOVE THE BRUSH, WAS AT THE OTHER END OF THE SPIT.

IT TOOK ME A GOODISH WHILE TO GET UP WITH IT, CRAWLING OFTEN ON ALL FOURS.

NIGHT HAD ALMOST COME WHEN I FOUND A LITTLE TENT OF GOATSKINS, WHICH HID BEN GUNN'S BOAT.

IT WAS A FRAMEWORK OF TOUGH WOOD AND STRETCHED UPON THAT A COVERING OF GOATSKIN, WITH THE HAIR INSIDE.

THE THING WAS EXTREMELY SMALL, EVEN FOR ME, AND I COULD HARDLY IMAGINE IT FLOATING WITH A FULL-SIZED MAN.

NOW THAT I HAD FOUND THE BOAT, YOU'D HAVE THOUGHT I'D HAD ENOUGH OF TRUANCY.

BUT, IN FACT, I HAD TAKEN ANOTHER NOTION AND BECOME SO FOND OF IT, I WOULD HAVE CARRIED IT IN THE TEETH OF CAPTAIN SMOLLETT HIMSELF.

THIS WAS TO SLIP OUT UNDER COVER OF THE NIGHT, CUT THE *HISPANIOLA* ADRIFT, AND LET HER GO ASHORE.

I WAS CONVINCED THAT, AFTER THEIR DEFEAT, THE MUTINEERS WOULD WANT TO CAST OFF AND THAT PREVENTING THEM WOULD BE A FINE THING.

DOWN I SAT TO WAIT FOR DARKNESS AND MADE A HEARTY MEAL OF BISCUIT.

IT WAS A NIGHT OUT OF TEN THOUSAND FOR MY PURPOSE. THE FOG HAD NOW BURIED ALL HEAVEN.

WHEN AT LAST I SHOULDERED THE CORACLE AND GROPED OUT OF MY SHELTER, THERE WERE BUT TWO POINTS VISIBLE.

ONE WAS THE GREAT FIRE ON SHORE, BY WHICH THE DEFEATED PIRATES LAY CAROUSING IN THE SWAMP.

THE OTHER, A MERE BLUR UPON THE DARKNESS, INDICATED THE POSITION OF THE ANCHORED SHIP.

HER BOW WAS NOW TOWARDS ME, AND WHAT I SAW WAS MERELY A REFLECTION ON THE FOG OF THE RAYS THAT FLOWED FROM THE CABIN.

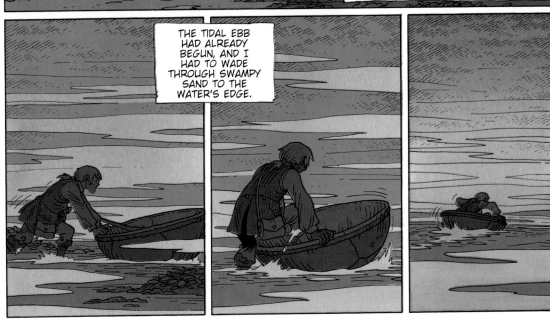

THE TIDAL EBB HAD ALREADY BEGUN, AND I HAD TO WADE THROUGH SWAMPY SAND TO THE WATER'S EDGE.

END OF PART TWO

ALL THE WHILE HEADING TOWARDS THE *HISPANIOLA*, I REMEMBERED THAT BEN GUNN HAD WARNED ME THAT THE CORACLE WAS "QUEER TO HANDLE TILL YOU KNEW HER WAY."

INDEED, SHE TURNED IN EVERY DIRECTION BUT THE ONE I WAS BOUND TO GO.

I AM VERY SURE I NEVER SHOULD HAVE MADE THE SHIP AT ALL BUT FOR THE TIDE.

BY GOOD FORTUNE, THE TIDE WAS SWEEPING ME DOWN.

FIRST SHE LOOMED BLACKER THAN DARKNESS AND, A SECOND LATER, I HAD LAID HOLD OF HER HAWSER.

THE HAWSER WAS AS TAUT AS A BOWSTRING, SO STRONG SHE PULLED UPON HER ANCHOR.

WERE I SO FOOLHARDY AS TO CUT HER FROM HER ANCHOR, I AND THE CORACLE WOULD BE KNOCKED CLEAN OUT OF THE WATER.

LUCKILY, A PUFF CAME, FORCED THE *HISPANIOLA* UP INTO THE CURRENT, AND I FELT THE HAWSER SLACKEN IN MY GRIP.

I OPENED MY GULLY WITH MY TEETH AND CUT ONE STRAND AFTER ANOTHER TILL THE VESSEL SWUNG ONLY BY TWO.

ALL THIS TIME I HAD HEARD THE SOUND OF LOUD VOICES FROM THE CABIN, BUT I HAD SCARCELY GIVEN EAR.

NOW I BEGAN TO PAY MORE HEED.

ONE I RECOGNIZED FOR ISRAEL HANDS'S, THAT HAD BEEN FLINT'S GUNNER IN FORMER DAYS. THE OTHER WAS, OF COURSE, MY FRIEND OF THE RED NIGHTCAP.

BOTH MEN WERE PLAINLY THE WORSE FOR DRINK, AS WAS PROVEN BY THE BOTTLE ONE OF THEM THREW OUT THE STERN WINDOW.

PLOUF

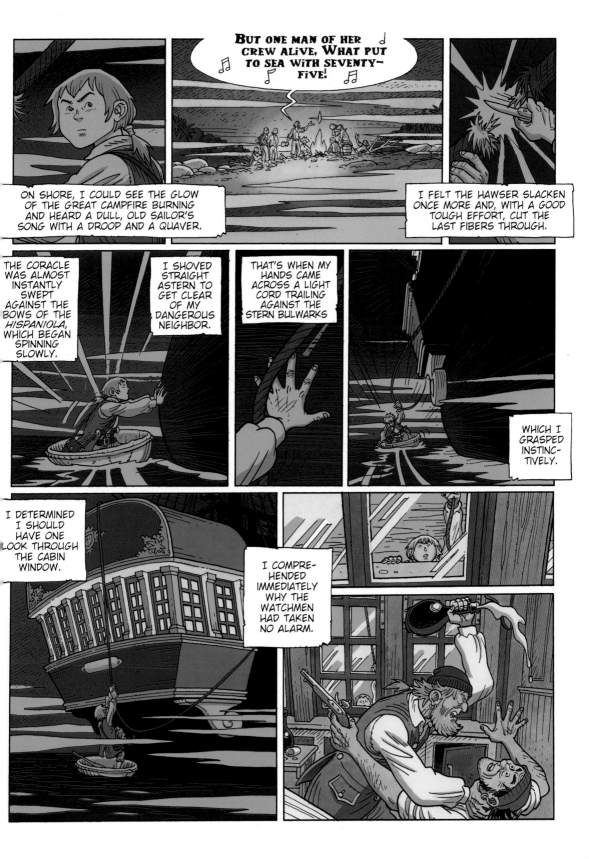

I DROPPED INTO THE CORACLE BEFORE LOSING MY BALANCE.

THE COMPANY ABOUT THE CAMPFIRE HAD BROKEN INTO THE CHORUS I'D HEARD SO OFTEN.

YO-HO-HO, ♪ AND A BOTTLE ♪ OF RUN!

THE CORACLE WHOSE SPEED HAD INCREASED, LURCHED SUDDENLY.

I GLANCED OVER MY SHOULDER, AND MY HEART JUMPED AGAINST MY RIBS, WHEN I REALIZED THE CURRENT HAD TURNED AT RIGHT ANGLES, NOW SWEEPING US TOWARDS THE OPEN SEA.

AT THE SAME MOMENT, I KNEW FROM THE NOISE ON BOARD THAT THE TWO DRUNK-ARDS HAD AWAK-ENED TO A SENSE OF THEIR DISASTER.

I LAY DOWN FLAT IN THAT WRETCHED SKIFF AND RECOM-MENDED MY SPIRIT TO ITS MAKER.

SO I MUST HAVE LAIN FOR HOURS, BEATEN UPON THE BILLOWS, WETTED WITH FLYING SPRAYS, EXPECTING DEATH.

GRADUALLY, WEARINESS OVERCAME MY TERRORS, AND I FELL ASLEEP DREAMING OF HOME AND THE "ADMIRAL BENBOW."

IT WAS BROAD DAY WHEN I AWOKE, TOSSING AT THE SOUTHWEST END OF THE ISLAND.

I WAS SCARCE A QUARTER MILE TO SEAWARD, AND IT WAS MY FIRST THOUGHT TO PADDLE IN AND LAND.

I SAW MYSELF, IF I VENTURED NEARER, DASHED TO DEATH UPON THE ROUGH SHORE.

NOT TO MENTION THE HUGE, SLIMY MONSTERS, WHICH I HAVE UNDERSTOOD SINCE WERE SEA LIONS AND ENTIRELY HARMLESS.

I REMEMBERED WHAT SILVER HAD SAID ABOUT THE CURRENT THAT SETS NORTHWARD ALONG THE WHOLE WEST COAST OF TREASURE ISLAND.

I RESERVED MY STRENGTH FOR AN ATTEMPT TO LAND UPON THE KINDLIER-LOOKING CAPE OF THE WOODS.

IT WAS PLAIN I MUSTN'T TRY TO GUIDE IT AND I SHOULD CONTENT MYSELF, IN SMOOTH PLACES, TO PADDLE OVER THE SIDE AND GIVER A SHOVE OR TWO TOWARD LAND.

I GREW SO BOLD AS TO TRY MY SKILL AT PADDLING, BUT WITH EVEN A SMALL CHANGE IN POSITION, THE CORACLE BEGAN TO PLUNGE INTO THE WAVES.

I SAW I MUST INFALLIBLY MISS THE CAPE OF THE WOODS, BUT I FELT SURE I SHOULD MAKE THE NEXT PROMONTORY.

I WAS, INDEED, CLOSE IN. I COULD SEE THE COOL, GREEN TREE-TOPS SWAYING TOGETHER IN THE BREEZE.

IT WAS HIGH TIME, FOR THE GLOW OF THE SUN AND SEA WATER HAD BURNED MY LIPS AND MADE MY BRAIN ACHE.

ALAS, THE CURRENT HAD SOON CARRIED ME PAST THE POINT, AND THAT WHEN I BEHELD A SIGHT...

RIGHT IN FRONT OF ME, THE *HISPANIOLA* UNDER SAIL.

HER SAILS WERE DRAWING AND, AS SHE WAS LYING A COURSE ABOUT NORTHWEST, I PRE-SUMED THE CREW WAS GOING ROUND THE ISLAND ON THEIR WAY BACK TO THE ANCHORAGE.

AND THEN SHE FELL RIGHT INTO THE WIND'S EYE AND STOOD THERE HELPLESS.

AFTER WHICH, SHE FELL AGAIN UPON ANOTHER TACK, SAILED FOR A MINUTE OR SO, AND BROUGHT UP ONCE MORE DEAD.

IT WAS PLAIN TO ME THAT NOBODY WAS STEERING

I THOUGHT PERHAPS, IF I COULD GET ON BOARD, I MIGHT RETURN THE VESSEL TO HER CAPTAIN.

IF ONLY I DARED TO SIT UP AND PADDLE, I MADE SURE THAT I COULD OVERHAUL HER.

I SET MYSELF, WITH ALL CAUTION, TO PADDLE AFTER THE UNSTEERED *HISPANIOLA*.

I GAINED SO RAPIDLY ON THE SCHOONER, I COULD SEE THE BRASS GLISTEN ON THE TILLER.

IT WAS PLAIN SHE WAS DESERTED. IF NOT, THE MEN WERE LYING DRUNK BELOW.

AT LAST I HAD MY CHANCE WHEN THE *HISPANIOLA*, THE CURRENT GRADUALLY TURNING HER, REVOLVED AND AT LAST PRESENTED ME HER STERN.

REDOUBLING MY EFFORTS, I BEGAN ONCE MORE TO OVERHAUL HER, WHEN THE WIND CAME AGAIN IN A CLAP AND PUSHED THE BOAT TOWARDS ME.

A DULL BLOW TOLD ME THAT THE SCHOONER HAD STRUCK THE CORACLE.

CRAK

I CLIMBED ONTO THE DECK, WHICH HAD NOT BEEN SWABBED SINCE THE MUTINY.

WHILE THE SHIP ROLLED AND PITCHED MUCH MORE THAN HAD MY OWN FRAIL CRAFT, I DISCOVERED THE TWO WATCHMEN.

REDCAP ON HIS BACK, WITH HIS ARMS LIKE A CRUCIFIX, HIS MOUTH AGAPE.

ISRAEL HANDS PROPPED AGAINST THE BULWARKS, HIS HANDS ON THE DECK, HIS FACE AS WHITE AS A CANDLE.

THERE WERE SPLASHES OF DARK BLOOD UPON THE PLANKS, AND I BEGAN TO FEEL SURE THEY WERE BOTH DEAD WHEN HANDS MADE A LOW MOAN.

COME ABOARD, MR. HANDS.

ARRRHH...BRR... BRANDY.

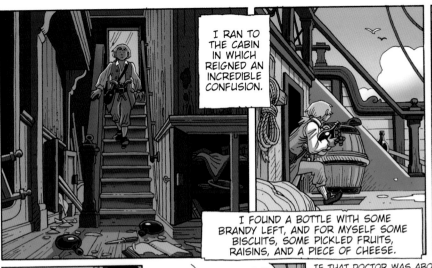

I RAN TO THE CABIN IN WHICH REIGNED AN INCREDIBLE CONFUSION.

I FOUND A BOTTLE WITH SOME BRANDY LEFT, AND FOR MYSELF SOME BISCUITS, SOME PICKLED FRUITS, RAISINS, AND A PIECE OF CHEESE.

THEN I WENT FOR A GOOD, DEEP DRINK OF WATER BEFORE HELPING HANDS.

GULP GULP

BY THUNDER, BUT I WANTED SOME O' THAT!

MUCH HURT?

IF THAT DOCTOR WAS ABOARD, I'D BE RIGHT ENOUGH IN A COUPLE OF TURNS. AS FOR THAT SWAB, HE'S GOOD AND DEAD. AND WHERE MOUGHT YOU HAVE COME FROM?

WELL, I'VE COME ABOARD TO TAKE POSSESSION OF THIS SHIP.

AND YOU'LL PLEASE REGARD ME AS YOUR CAPTAIN!

I CAN'T HAVE THESE COLORS, AND BY YOUR LEAVE, I'LL STRIKE 'EM.

THERE'S AN END TO CAPTAIN SILVER.

YOU GIVES ME FOOD AND DRINK, AND OLD SCARF TO TIE MY WOUND UP, AND I'LL TELL YOU HOW TO SAIL HER.

I RECKON, CAP'N HAWKINS, YOU'LL KIND OF WANT TO GET ASHORE, NOW.

I'LL TELL YOU ONE THING. I MEAN TO GET INTO NORTH INLET, AND BEACH HER QUIETLY THERE.

TO BE SURE YOU DID! I CAN SEE, CAN'T I? WHY, I HAVEN'T NO CH'ICE, NOT I!

IN THREE MINUTES I HAD THE *HISPANIOLA* SAILING ALONG THE COAST OF TREASURE ISLAND, WITH GOOD HOPES OF TURNING THE NORTHERN POINT ERE NOON.

THEN I LASHED THE TILLER, WENT BELOW TO LOOK FOR A HANDKERCHIEF AND HELPED HANDS BANDAGE HIS WOUND.

AFTER HE HAD EATEN A LITTLE AND HAD A SWALLOW MORE OF BRANDY, HE BEGAN TO PICK UP VISIBLY, SPOKE LOUDER AND CLEARER, AND LOOKED IN EVERY WAY ANOTHER MAN.

WE PASSED A LOW, SANDY COUNTRY AND SOON TURNED THE CORNER OF THE ROCKY HILL THAT ENDS THE ISLAND ON THE NORTH.

I WAS GREATLY ELATED, AND MY CONSCIENCE, SMITTEN HARD BY MY DESERTION, WAS QUIETED BY THE GREAT CONQUEST I HAD MADE.

ALL WOULD HAVE BEEN PERFECT BUT FOR HANDS AND THAT ODD SMILE MIXING ALL AT ONCE PAIN, WEAKNESS, AND TREACHERY.

HE CRAFTILY WATCHED, AND WATCHED, AND WATCHED ME AT MY WORK.

CAP'N, S'POSE YOU WAS TO HEAVE O'BRIEN OVERBOARD?

I'M NOT STRONG ENOUGH, AND THERE HE LIES, FOR ME.

YOU KNOW WHAT, JIM? I'LL TAKE IT KIND IF YOU'D GO FIND ME A BOTTLE OF--

--A--WELL, A--I CAN'T HIT THE NAME ON'T.

A BOTTLE OF...OF WINE! YES, THAT'S IT!!

THIS HERE BRANDY'S TOO STRONG FOR MY HEAD.

THE COXSWAIN'S HESITATION SEEMED TO BE UNNATURAL. THE WHOLE STORY WAS A PRETEXT, FOR HE WANTED ME TO LEAVE THE DECK.

AFTER SLIPPING OFF MY SHOES, I RAN QUIETLY DOWN TO THE FORECASTLE LADDER.

THIS WAS ALL THAT I REQUIRED TO KNOW. ISRAEL COULD MOVE ABOUT; HE WAS NOW ARMED.

IT WAS PLAIN THAT I WAS MEANT TO BE THE VICTIM.

WHEN I ARRIVED WITH MY BOTTLE OF WINE, HANDS LAY AS I HAD LEFT HIM.

HERE'S LUCK!

AH, JIM!! I FEEL CLOSE TO MY END, I FEEL IT.

IF I WAS YOU, I WOULD GO TO MY PRAYERS.

WHY?

WHY? YOU'VE BROKEN YOUR TRUST; YOU'VE LIVED IN SIN AND LIES AND BLOOD.

FOR GOD'S MERCY, THAT'S WHY.

FOR THIRTY YEARS I'VE SAILED THE SEAS AND I NEVER SEEN GOOD COME O' GOODNESS YET.

HIM AS STRIKES FIRST IS MY FANCY, AMEN, SO BE IT.

YOU JUST TAKE MY ORDERS, CAP'N HAWKINS, AND WE'LL SAIL SLAP IN AND BE DONE WITH IT.

THE NAVIGATION WAS DELICATE AND THE ENTRANCE NARROW, BUT HANDS WAS AN EXCELLENT PILOT.

SO HE EXPLAINED TO ME HOW TO BEACH THE SHIP, THEN TO GET HER OFF AGAIN, AND I BREATHLESSLY OBEYED HIS COMMANDS.

SO MUCH SO I ENDED RELAXING THE WATCH I HAD KEPT HITHERTO.

I MIGHT HAVE FALLEN WITHOUT A STRUGGLE HAD NOT A SUDDEN DISQUIETUDE MADE ME TURN MY HEAD.

AAH!!

RRAAH!!

HAA!

THE PRIMING WAS TOO HUMID.

I CURSED MYSELF FOR NOT HAVING REPRIMED AND RELOADED MY ONLY WEAPONS.

MY HEART HAD NEVER BEAT SO WILDLY AS NOW, AND YET, AGAINST AN ELDERLY, WOUNDED SEAMAN, I STILL HAD A CHANCE.

AND THEN SUDDENLY ...

BONK

THE *HISPANIOLA*, WHICH HAD JUST STRUCK, SWIFTLY CANTED OVER TO THE PORTSIDE.

AAAH!

MFFF!!

OUCH!

BLOW AND ALL, I WAS THE FIRST AFOOT AGAIN, FOR HANDS HAD GOT INVOLVED WITH THE DEAD BODY.

THE CANTING DECK WAS NO PLACE FOR RUNNING, SO I SPRANG INTO THE MIZZEN SHROUDS.

TCHAC

I LOST NO TIME IN CHANGING THE PRIMING OF MY PISTOLS.

AFTER HESITATING, HANDS ALSO HAULED HIMSELF HEAVILY INTO THE SHROUDS WITH NO END OF TIME AND GROANS.

ONE MORE STEP, MR. HANDS, AND I'LL BLOW YOUR BRAINS OUT.

JIM, I RECKON WE'VE FOULED, YOU AND ME, AND WE'LL HAVE TO SIGN ARTICLES.

"I RECKON I'LL HAVE TO STRIKE, WHICH COMES HARD, YOU SEE, FOR A MASTER MARINER TO A SHIP'S YOUNKER LIKE YOU.

AAH!

BLAM BLAM

AAH!

BLOUTCH

HANDS ROSE ONCE TO THE SURFACE IN A LATHER OF FOAM AND BLOOD, AND THEN SANK AGAIN FOR GOOD.

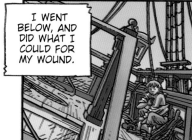

IT WAS MY FIRST THOUGHT TO PLUCK FORTH THE DIRK, BUT I DESISTED WITH A VIOLENT SHUDDER.

ODDLY ENOUGH, THAT VERY SHUDDER DID THE BUSINESS, FOR THE KNIFE HELD ME BY A MERE PINCH OF SKIN.

I WENT BELOW, AND DID WHAT I COULD FOR MY WOUND.

I TOOK O'BRIEN LIKE A SACK OF BRAN AND TUMBLED HIM OVERBOARD.

BLOUF

FINALLY, HOLDING THE CUT HAWSER, I LET MYSELF DROP OVERBOARD AND WADED ASHORE.

ABOUT THE SAME TIME, THE SUN WENT FAIRLY DOWN AND THE BREEZE WHISTLED LOW AMONG THE TOSSING PINES.

AT LAST, I WAS OFF THE SEA, NOR HAD I RETURNED THENCE EMPTY-HANDED AND I HOPED THAT EVEN CAPTAIN SMOLLETT WOULD CONFESS I HAD NOT LOST MY TIME.

SO IN FAMOUS SPIRITS I WENT ROUND THE TWO-PEAKED HILL, HOMEWARD FOR THE BLOCKHOUSE.

ARRIVING NEAR TO WHERE I HAD ENCOUNTERED BEN GUNN, I NOTICED WITH WONDER THE GLOW OF THE FIRE BEFORE WHICH HE MUST BE COOKING HIS SUPPER.

THE NIGHTFALL HAD RENDERED MY PROGRESS DIFFICULT, WHEN THE GLIMMER OF THE MOON FINALLY SPILLED OVER ME.

WITH THIS TO HELP ME, I PASSED RAPIDLY TOWARDS THE STOCKADE, SOMETIMES WALKING, SOMETIMES RUNNING.

THOUGH I WENT A TRIFLE WARILY, A GLOW OF RED COLOR APPEARED AMONG THE TREES.

WHEN I ARRIVED AT THE EDGE OF THE CLEARING, I SAW THAT AN IMMENSE FIRE HAS BURNED ITSELF TO EMBERS BESIDE THE HOUSE.

I STOPPED, ASTONISHED, FOR THE CAPTAIN'S ORDERS WERE TO BE SPARING OF FIREWOOD.

I CROSSED THE PALISADE, CRAWLED TOWARD THE HOUSE, AND FELT A KEEN SOOTHING AT HEARING MY FRIENDS SNORING TOGETHER.

WITH MY ARMS BEFORE ME I WALKED STEADILY IN TO LIE DOWN, CHUCKLING AT THE THOUGHT OF THEIR FACES WHEN THEY FOUND ME IN THE MORNING.

MY FOOT STRUCK A SLEEPER'S LEG, AND HE TURNED AND GROANED BUT WITHOUT AWAKENING.

THEN, ALL OF THE SUDDEN--

PIECES OF EIGHT! PIECES OF EIGHT!

SILVER'S GREEN PARROT, CAPTAIN FLINT, THUS ANNOUNCED MY ARRIVAL WITH HER WEARISOME REFRAIN.

I HAD NO TIME LEFT ME TO RECOVER, FOR THE SLEEPERS AWOKE.

PIECES OF EIGHT! PIECES OF EIGHT!

WHO GOES?

I TURNED TO RUN, STRUCK AGAINST ONE PERSON, AND RAN FULL INTO ANOTHER'S ARMS.

BRING A TORCH, DICK.

THE RED GLARE OF THE TORCH SHOWED ME THE PIRATES WERE IN POSSESSION OF THE HOUSE AND STORES.

AND WORST OF ALL, NOT A SIGN OF ANY PRISONER. MY HEART SMOTE ME SORELY THAT I HAD NOT BEEN THERE TO PERISH WITH THEM.

SO, HERE'S JIM HAWKINS, SHIVER ME TIMBERS! DROPPED IN LIKE, EH?

THERE WERE SIX OF THE BUCCANEERS, ALL TOLD, ONE OF WHOM WHOSE HEAD WAS GRAVELY WOUNDED.

QUITE A PLEASANT SURPRISE.

I ALWAYS KNEW YOU WERE SMART, BUT THIS HERE TOPS IT ALL.

YOUR FRIENDS ARE FURIOUS WITH YOU, THE DOCTOR CALLS YOU AN "UNGRATEFUL SCAMP." YOU CAN'T GO BACK TO YOUR OWN LOT.

YOU'LL HAVE TO JINE WITH CAP'N SILVER.

IF YOU LIKE THE SERVICE, WELL, YOU'LL JINE.

AND IF YOU DON'T, YOU'RE FREE TO ANSWER NO.

WELL, IF I'M TO CHOOSE, I DECLARE I HAVE A RIGHT TO KNOW WHAT'S WHAT, AND WHY YOU'RE HERE, AND WHERE MY FRIENDS ARE.

YESTERDAY MORNING, DOWN CAME DR. LIVESEY TO PARLEY. SAYS HE, "CAP'N SILVER, YOU'RE SOLD OUT. SHIP'S GONE."

WE BARGAINED, HIM AND I: STORES, BLOCKHOUSE, THE FIREWOOD YOU CUT, AND THE WHOLE BLESSED BOAT.

AS FOR THEM, THEY'VE TRAMPED; I DON'T KNOW WHERE'S THEY ARE, BUT NOT BEFORE THE DOCTOR TOLD US, AS FOR YOU, "CONFOUND HIM, WE'RE ABOUT SICK OF HIM."

WELL, IT'S ALL THAT YOU'RE TO HEAR, MY SON.

BUT THERE'S A THING OF TWO I HAVE TO TELL YOU.

I WAS IN THE APPLE BARREL THE NIGHT WE SIGHTED LAND, AND I HEARD YOU, JOHN, AND YOU, JOHNSON, AND I TOLD EVERY WORD YOU SAID.

AS FOR THE SCHOONER, IT WAS I WHO CUT HER CABLE, WHO KILLED THE MEN YOU HAD ABOARD OF HER, AND WHO BROUGHT HER WHERE YOU'LL NEVER SEE HER MORE.

I'VE HAD THE TOP OF THIS BUSINESS FROM THE FIRST; I NO MORE FEAR YOU THAN I FEAR A FLY.

KILL ME, IF YOU PLEASE, OR SPARE ME, BUT ONE THING I'LL SAY, IF YOU SPARE ME, I'LL SAVE YOU ALL I CAN FROM THE GALLOWS.

IT WAS HIM THAT KNOWED BLACK DOG!!

AND THAT FAKED THE CHART FROM BILLY BONES.

THEN HERE GOES!

AVAST, THERE!

MAYBE YOU THOUGHT YOU WAS CAP'N HERE, TOM MORGAN?

TOM'S RIGHT.

I STOOD HAZING LONG ENOUGH FROM THE CAPTAIN. I'LL BE HANGED IF I'LL BE HAZED BY YOU, JOHN SILVER.

DID ANY OF YOU GENTLEMAN WANT TO HAVE IT OUT WITH ME?

TAKE A CUTLASS, HIM THAT DARES, AND I'LL SEE THE COLOR OF HIS INSIDES, CRUTCH AND ALL!

THAT'S YOUR SORT, IS IT? I'M CAP'N HERE BECAUSE I'M THE BEST MAN BY A LONG SEA MILE. YOU WON'T FIGHT, AS GENTLEMAN O' FORTUNE SHOULD; THEN, BY THUNDER, YOU'LL OBEY.

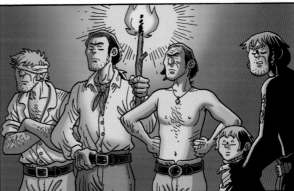

THAT BOY'S MORE A MAN THAN ANY PAIR OF RATS OF YOU IN THIS HERE HOUSE. LET ME SEE HIM THAT'LL LAY A HAND ON HIM!

THERE WAS A LONG PAUSE AFTER THIS, WHILE MY HEART BEAT LIKE A SLEDGE HAMMER, FOLLOWING WHICH, THE MEN DREW GRADUALLY TOGETHER TOWARD THE FAR END OF THE BLOCKHOUSE AND BEGAN WHISPERING WHILE TURNING THEIR EYES TOWARD THE SEA COOK.

THEY DECIDED TO STEP OUTSIDE FOR A COUNCIL AND WENT OUT, ONE AFTER THE OTHER, EACH ADDING SOME APOLOGY TO SILVER.

LOOK YOU HERE, JIM HAWKINS.  YOU'RE WITHIN HALF A PLANK OF DEATH, OR A LONG SIGHT WORSE, OF TORTURE.

THEY'RE GOING TO THROW ME OFF. BUT, YOU MARK, I STAND BY YOU THROUGH THICK AND THIN.

BUT I SEE YOU WAS THE RIGHT SORT. I SAYS TO MYSELF: "YOU STAND BY HAWKINS, JOHN, AND HAWKINS'LL STAND BY YOU. YOU'RE HIS LAST CARD, AND HE'S YOURS!"

YOU MEAN ALL'S LOST?

AYE, BY GUM, I DID! SHIP GONE, NECK GONE--THAT'S THE SIZE OF IT.

I'LL SAVE YOUR LIFE FROM THEM, IF SO BE AS I CAN, BUT TIT FOR TAT.

YOU SAVE LONG JOHN FROM SWINGING.

WHAT I CAN DO, THAT I'LL DO.

IT'S A BARGAIN.

BY THUNDER, I'M ON SQUIRE'S SIDE NOW.

HOW YOU DONE IT, I DON'T KNOW, BUT I KNOW YOU'VE GOT THAT SHIP SAFE SOMEWHERES. I KNOW WHEN A GAME'S UP.

AH, YOU THAT'S YOUNG--

YOU AND ME MIGHT HAVE A POWER OF GOOD TOGETHER!

AND TALKING O' TROUBLE, WHY DID THAT DOCTOR GIVE ME THIS CHART, JIM?

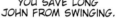

WELL, NOW, I'LL ANSWER THESE FOUR POINTS.

YOU ALL KNOW IF YOU'D LISTENED TO ME, WE'D 'A' BEEN ABOARD THE *HISPANIOLA* THIS NIGHT AS EVER WAS, EVERY MAN ALIVE, AND FIT, AND THE TREASURE IN THE HOLD OF HER.

WHO FORCED MY HAND? WHO TIPPED ME THE BLACK SPOT THE DAY WE LANDED AND BEGAN THIS DANCE?

BUT WHO DONE IT? WHY, IT WAS ANDERSON, AND HANDS, AND YOU, GEORGE MERRY! AND YOU HAVE THE INSOLENCE TO STAND FOR CAP'N FOR ME--YOU, THAT SANK THE LOT OF US!

I'M SICK TO SPEAK TO YOU OTHERS! GENTLEMEN O' FORTUNE! I RECKON TAILORS IS YOUR TRADE.

AH! WE'RE THAT NEAR THE GIBBET THAT MY NECK'S STIFF WITH THINKING ON IT.

AND THAT BOY--

ISN'T HE A HOSTAGE? HE MIGHT BE OUR LAST CHANCE, AND I SHOULDN'T WONDER.

AND THE DOCTOR? YOU'RE MIGHTY HAPPY THAT HE COMES TO SEE YOU! AND THAT THERE'S A RESCUE SHIP ON THE WAY? MAYBE YOU KNEW THAT?

COME OVER HERE A LITTLE.

YOU LOOK THERE!

POF

YES, THAT'S FLINT'S, SURE ENOUGH.

MIGHTY PRETTY, BUT HOW ARE WE TO GET AWAY WITH IT, AND US NO SHIP?

NOW I GIVE YOU WARNING, GEORGE. ONE MORE WORD OF YOUR SAUCE, AND I'LL FIGHT YOU. AND NOW I RESIGN, BY THUNDER!

I'M FED UP WITH BEING YOUR CAP'N.

NO!! BARBEQUE FOR CAP'N! SILVER!

SO THAT'S THE TOON, IS IT?

GEORGE, I RECKON YOU'LL HAVE TO WAIT ANOTHER TURN, FRIEND.

AND LUCKY FOR YOU ALL AS I'M NOT A REVENGEFUL MAN.

HERE, JIM! A CUR'OSITY FOR YOU.

THE PRINTED SIDE HAD BEEN BLACKENED WITH WOOD ASH; ON THE BLANK SIDE HAD BEEN WRITTEN "DEPPOSED."

THAT WAS THE END OF THE NIGHT'S BUSINESS.

WITH A DRINK ALL ROUND, WE LAY DOWN TO SLEEP, AND THE OUTSIDE OF SILVER'S VENGEANCE WAS TO PUT GEORGE UP FOR SENTINEL.

IT WAS LONG ERE I COULD CLOSE AN EYE, WHEREAS SILVER SNORED ALOUD.

RRRZZZZZRRRZZ

YET MY HEART WAS SORE FOR HIM TO THINK WHAT AWAITED HIM.

BLOCKHOUSE, AHOY! HERE'S THE DOCTOR.

WE WERE ALL AWAKENED BY THAT CLEAR, HEARTY VOICE HAILING US FROM THE MARGIN OF THE WOOD.

YOU, DOCTOR! TOP O' THE MORNING TO YOU!

I REMEMBERED MY INSUBORDINATION AND STEALTHY CONDUCT AND FELT ASHAMED TO LOOK HIM IN THE FACE.

BRIGHT AND EARLY TO BE SURE GEORGE, HELP DR. LIVESEY OVER THE SHIP'S SIDE!

ALL A-DOIN' WELL, YOUR PATIENTS WAS. WE'VE QUITE A SURPRISE FOR YOU, TOO, SIR.

A NOO BOARDER AND LODGER; SLEP' LIKE A SUPERCARGO, RIGHT ALONGSIDE OF JOHN.

NOT JIM?

THE VERY SAME.

WITH ONE GRIM NOD TO ME, HE PROCEEDED WITH HIS WORK AMONG THE SICK, RATTLING ON AS IF HE WERE PAYING AN ORDINARY VISIT AND NOT AS IF HIS LIFE DEPENDED ON A HAIR.

WELL, WELL, DUTY FIRST AND PLEASURE AFTERWARD.

AFTER HE HAD DOSED THEM ROUND, AND THEY HAD TAKEN HIS PRESCRIPTIONS LIKES CHARITY SCHOOL CHILDREN, HE TURNED TOWARDS ME.

AND NOW I SHOULD WISH TO HAVE A TALK WITH THAT BOY, PLEASE.

SI-LENCE! DOCTOR, WE'RE ALL HUMBLY GRATEFUL FOR YOUR KINDNESS, AND KNOW AS HOW YOU HAD A FANCY FOR THE BOY.

JIM, WILL YOU GIVE ME YOUR WORD OF HONOR NOT TO SLIP YOUR CABLE?

I GIVE YOU MY PLEDGE.

SLOW, LAD, SLOW. THEY MIGHT ROUND UPON US, IF WE WAS SEEN TO HURRY.

DOCTOR, THE BOY'LL TELL YOU HOW I SAVED HIS LIFE AT THE PERIL OF MY OWN.

AND YOU'LL SPEAK ME FAIR, DOCTOR, AND GIVE ME A BIT O' HOPE TO GO ON?

WHY, JOHN, YOU'RE NOT AFRAID?

I'M NO COWARD, BUT I'VE THE SHAKES UPON ME FOR THE GALLOWS.

YOU'RE A GOOD MAN AND TRUE. AND YOU'LL NOT FORGET WHAT I HAVE DONE FOR GOOD, NOT ANYMORE THAN THE BAD. AND NOW, I LEAVE YOU AND JIM ALONE.

SO SAYING, HE STEPPED BACK AND SAT DOWN UPON A TREE STUMP, SO AS TO COMMAND A SIGHT OF ME AND THE DOCTOR AND, AT THE SAME TIME, OF HIS UNRULY RUFFI-ANS WHO WERE REKINDLING THE FIRE AND MAKING THE BREAKFAST.

SO, JIM, AS YOU HAVE BREWED, SO SHALL YOU DRINK, MY BOY. IT WAS DOWNRIGHT COWARDLY TO HAVE GONE OFF WHEN THE CAPTAIN WAS ILL.

DOCTOR, I HAVE BLAMED MYSELF ENOUGH.

I CAN DIE, BUT WHAT I FEAR IS TORTURE.

JIM, I CAN'T HAVE THIS. WHIP OVER, AND WE'LL RUN FOR IT.

I PASSED MY WORD.

I KNOW, BUT I'LL TAKE IT ON MY SHOULDERS. COME ON, JUMP!

NO. SILVER TRUSTED ME; I PASSED MY WORD.

BUT YOU DID NOT LET ME FINISH: I GOT THE SHIP, SHE LIES IN NORTH INLET, JUST BELOW HIGH WATER, AT HALF TIDE HIGH AND DRY.

RAPIDLY I DESCRIBED TO HIM MY ADVENTURES.

EVERY STEP, IT'S YOU THAT SAVES OUR LIVES.

YOU FOUND OUT THE PLOT; YOU FOUND BEN GUNN. OH! TALKING OF BEN--

SILVER! OH, SILVER!

I'LL GIVE YOU A PIECE OF ADVICE: DON'T YOU BE IN ANY GREAT HURRY AFTER THAT TREASURE.

AND LOOK OUT FOR SQUALLS WHEN YOU FIND IT.

SIR, THAT'S TOO MUCH AND TOO LITTLE. YOU LEFT THE BLOCKHOUSE, YOU'VE GIVEN ME THAT THERE CHART, AND ALL WITH NO EXPLANATION. THIS HERE'S TOO MUCH.

NO, I'VE NO RIGHT TO SAY MORE. SILVER, IF WE BOTH GET ALIVE OUT OF THIS WOLF TRAP, I'LL DO MY BEST TO SAVE YOU.

ONE LAST PIECE OF ADVICE: KEEP THE BOY CLOSE BESIDE YOU, AND WHEN YOU NEED HELP, HALLOO.

GOOD-BYE, JIM.

DR. LIVESEY SHOOK HANDS WITH ME AND SET OFF AT A BRISK PACE INTO THE WOOD.

JIM, IF I SAVED YOUR LIFE, YOU SAVED MINE; AND I'LL NOT FORGET IT.

AND NOW, WE'RE TO GO IN FOR THIS HERE TREASURE HUNTING--

--AND YOU AND ME MUST STICK CLOSE, IF WE'RE TO SAVE OUR NECKS.

JUST THEN A MAN HAILED US THAT BREAKFAST WAS READY, WE WENT TO EAT THE BISCUIT AND BACON, BEFORE A FIRE FIT TO ROAST AN OX.

AYE, MATES, IT'S LUCKY YOU HAVE BARBEQUE TO THINK FOR YOU WITH THIS HERE HEAD.

I GOT WHAT I WANTED.

THEY MAY HAVE THE SHIP, BUT WE HAVE THE CHART--AND THE BOATS.

I'LL TAKE HIM IN A LINE, BUT ONCE WE GET THE SHIP AND TREASURE BOTH, WHY, THEN, WE'LL TALK MR. HAWKINS OVER.

IF THE MEN WERE IN A GOOD HUMOR, FOR MY PART I WAS HORRIBLY CAST DOWN.

SILVER HAD STILL A FOOT IN EITHER CAMP, AND SHOULD THE SCHEME PROVED FEASIBLE, WOULD NOT HESITATE TO BETRAY ME.

AND EVEN THEN WHAT DANGER LAY BEFORE US!

ADD TO THIS THE MYSTERY THAT STILL HUNG OVER THE BEHAVIOR OF MY FRIENDS AND THE DOCTOR'S LAST WARNING.

THUS IT WAS WITH AN UNEASY HEART THAT I SET FORTH BEHIND MY CAPTORS ON THE QUEST FOR TREASURE.

WE MADE A CURIOUS FIGURE, FOR SILVER HAD TWO GUNS SLUNG ABOUT HIM, BESIDES THE GREAT CUTLASS AT HIS WAIST AND A PISTOL IN EACH POCKET, AND CAPTAIN FLINT SAT PERCHED UPON HIS SHOULDER, AND ME, WHOM HE HELD ON A LEASH, LED LIKE A DANCING BEAR.

THE OTHER MEN WERE VARIOUSLY BURDENED, SOME CARRYING PICKS AND SHOVELS, OTHER LADEN WITH PROVISIONS AND BRANDY FOR THE MIDDAY MEAL.

WE STRAGGLED TO THE BEACH, WHERE THE TWO GIGS AWAITED US. EVEN THESE BORE TRACE OF THE DRUNKEN FOLLY OF THE PIRATES. WE SET FORTH UPON THE BOSOM OF THE ANCHORAGE.

AS WE PULLED OVER, THERE WAS SOME DISCUSSION ON THE CHART AND THE "TALL TREE" MENTIONED BY FLINT.

THE TOP OF THE PLATEAU WAS DOTTED THICKLY WITH PINE TREES, CERTAIN OF WHICH, OF A DIFFERENT SPECIES, ROSE CLEAR ABOVE THE OTHERS.

EVERY MAN ON BOARD HAD PICKED A FAVORITE OF HIS OWN ERE WE WERE HALFWAY OVER.

AFTER QUITE A LONG PASSAGE, WE LANDED AT THE MOUTH OF THE RIVER WHICH RUNS DOWN A CLEFT OF THE SPYGLASS.

THENCE, WE BEGAN TO ASCEND TOWARD THE PLATEAU.

HEAVY, MIRY GROUND SLOWLY GAVE WAY TO A MORE PLEASANT PORTION OF THE ISLAND.

THE AIR WAS FRESH AND SCENTED WITH THE AROMAS OF FLOWERING SHRUBS AND GREEN NUTMEG, WHILE THE SUNBEAMS REFRESHED US.

THE PARTY SPREAD IN A FAN SHAPE, AND SILVER PLOWED ALONG. FROM TIME TO TIME, INDEED, I HAD TO LEND HIM A HAND.

WHEN SUDDENLY ...

AAAH!!

HE WAS A SEAMAN.

YOU WOULDN'T LOOK TO A FIND A BISHOP HERE, I RECKON?

HIS FEET POINTING IN ONE DIRECTION, HIS HANDS, RAISED ABOVE HIS HEAD LIKE A DIVER'S--THE SKELETON WASN'T IN A NATURAL POSITION.

I'VE TAKEN A NOTION THAT HERE'S THE COMPASS. JUST TAKE A BEARING.

THE BODY POINTED STRAIGHT IN THE DIRECTION OF THE ISLAND, AND THE COMPASS READ DULY E.S.E. AND BY E.

I THOUGHT SO; THIS HERE IS A P'INTER, BUT IT MAKES ME COLD INSIDE.

FLINT KILLED THE SIX, EVERY MAN; AND THIS ONE HE HAULED HERE AND LAID DOWN BY COMPASS.

THEY'RE LONG BONES AND THE HAIR'S BEEN YELLOW. THAT WOULD BE ALLARDYCE.

AYE, HE OWED ME MONEY, HE DID, AND TOOK MY KNIFE ASHORE.

SPEAKING OF KNIVES, WHERE'S HIS'N? THE BIRDS WOULD LEAVE IT BE.

THERE AIN'T A THING LEFT HERE, NOT A COPPER DOIT NOR A BACCY BOX.

GREAT GUNS! MESSMATES, BUT IF FLINT WAS LIVING, THIS WOULD BE A HOT SPOT FOR YOU AND ME.

I SAW HIM DEAD WITH THESE HERE DEADLIGHTS.

NOW HE HOLLERED FOR THE RUM AND NOW HE SANG "FIFTEEN MEN."

THE DEATHHAUL WAS ALREADY ON 'IM.

COME, COME, STOW THIS TALK. FETCH AHEAD FOR THE DOUBLOONS.

IN SPITE OF THE HOT SUN AND DAYLIGHT, THE PIRATES STARTED OFF, SPEAKING WITH BATED BREATH.

THE TERROR OF FLINT HAD FALLEN ON THEIR SPIRITS.

THE WHOLE PARTY SAT DOWN AS SOON AS THEY GAINED THE BROW OF THE ASCENT.

THERE WAS NO SOUND BUT THAT OF THE DISTANT BREAKERS, THE CHIRP OF INSECTS IN THE BRUSH; THE VERY LARGENESS OF THE VIEW INCREASED THE SENSE OF SOLITUDE.

SILVER TOOK BEARINGS WITH HIS COMPASS.

THERE ARE THREE "TALL TREES" ABOUT IN THE RIGHT LINE FROM SKELETON ISLAND. "SPYGLASS SHOULDER" MEANS THAT LOWER P'INT THERE.

IT'S CHILD'S PLAY TO FIND THE STUFF NOW. I'VE HALF A MIND TO DINE FIRST.

THINKING OF FLINT HAS DONE ME.

YOU PRAISE YOUR STARS HE'S DEAD.

IT WAS THE RUM THAT TOOK HIM--BLUE IN THE FACE, TOO.

EVER SINCE THEY HAD FOUND THE SKELETON, THEY HAD SPOKEN LOWER AND LOWER, ALMOST WHISPERING, HARDLY INTERRUPTING THE SILENCE OF THE WOOD.

FIFTEEN MEN ON THE DEAD MAN'S CHEST

YO-HO-HO, AND A BOTTLE OF RUM!

THE SONG HAD BROKEN OFF IN THE MIDDLE OF A NOTE, AS THOUGH SOMEONE HAD LAID HIS HAND UPON THE SINGER'S MOUTH.

IT'S FLINT, BY--!

COME--I CAN'T NAME THE VOICE, BUT IT'S SOMEONE SKYLARKING, YOU MAY LAY TO THAT.

THEIR COURAGE AND COLOR HAD COME BACK WHEN

DARBY M'GRAW!! DARBY M'GRAW RUM, DARBY!

THEY WAS HIS LAST WORDS.

THAT FIXES IT! LET'S GO.

SHIPMATES, I'M HERE TO GET THAT STUFF, AND I'LL NOT BE BEAT BY MAN NOR DEVIL.

I NEVER WAS FEARED OF FLINT IN HIS LIFE AND, BY THE POWERS, I'LL FACE HIM DEAD.

BELAY THERE, JOHN! DON'T YOU CROSS A SPERRIT.

IT WAS LIKE FLINT'S VOICE, BUT NOT JUST SO CLEAR-AWAY LIKE IT--IT WAS LIKER SOMEBODY ELSE--IT WAS LIKER BEN GUNN--

AYE, AND SO IT WERE. BEN GUNN IT WERE!

IT DON'T MAKE MUCH ODDS, DO IT, NOW? THEY'RE BOTH DEAD THE TWO OF 'EM.

SOON THEY WERE CHATTING TOGETHER, THEN SHOULDERED THEIR TOOLS AND SET FORTH AGAIN.

MERRY WAS WALKING FIRST WITH THE COMPASS TO KEEP THEM ON THE RIGHT LINE WITH SKELETON ISLAND. DICK ALONE STILL HELD HIS BIBLE.

IT WAS FINE OPEN WALKING HERE. OUR WAY LAY A LITTLE DOWNHILL, FOR THE PLATEAU TILTED TOWARD THE WEST.

THE FIRST OF THE TALL TREES WAS REACHED, AND BY THE BEARING PROVED THE WRONG ONE.

SO WITH THE SECOND.

THE THIRD ROSE NEARLY TWO HUNDRED FEET INTO THE AIR, WITH A RED COLUMN AS BIG AS A COTTAGE.

BUT IT WAS NOT ITS SIZE THAT IMPRESSED MY COMPANIONS.

IT WAS THE KNOWLEDGE THAT SEVEN HUNDRED THOUSAND POUNDS IN GOLD LAY SOMEWHERE BURIED BELOW.

THE THOUGHT SWALLOWED UP THEIR TERRORS, THEIR FEET GREW SPEEDIER.

SILVER HOBBLED ON HIS CRUTCH, CURSED LIKE A MADMAN, PLUCKED AT THE LINE THAT HELD ME TO HIM, WHILE GIVING ME DEADLY LOOKS.

AS FOR ME, I WAS HAUNTED BY THE TRAGEDY THAT HAD BEEN ACTED HERE AND I THOUGHT I COULD HEAR THE RINGING CRIES OF THE SIX ACCOMPLICES CUT DOWN BY THE BUCCANEER WITH THE BLUE FACE.

THE NEARNESS OF THE GOLD HAD MADE HIM FORGET HIS PROMISE TO THE DOCTOR AND TO RENEW HIS PLAN TO CUT EVERY HONEST THROAT, BEFORE SAILING AWAY WITH THE RICHES.

DICK, WHO HAD DROPPED BEHIND, WAS BABBLING TO HIMSELF BOTH PRAYERS AND CURSES.

CERTAINLY HE TOOK NO PAINS TO HIDE HIS THOUGHTS.

HUZZA, MATES, ALL TOGETHER!

ALL WAS CLEAR. THE SEVEN HUNDRED THOUSAND POUNDS WERE GONE!

SILVER, WHO HAD JUST LOST EVERYTHING, REACTED IMMEDIATELY.

WE PUT THE HOLLOW BETWEEN US TWO AND THE OTHER FIVE. HIS LOOKS WERE NOW QUITE FRIENDLY.

JIM, TAKE THAT, AND STAND BY FOR TROUBLE.

SO YOU'VE CHANGED SIDES AGAIN.

THE BUCCANEERS HAD LEAPT INTO THE PIT AND WERE DIGGING WITH THEIR FINGERS.

LOOK!

TWO GUINEAS! THAT'S YOUR SEVEN HUNDRED THOUSAND POUNDS, IS IT?

THAT MAN THERE KNEW IT ALL ALONG. YOU'LL SEE IT WROTE THERE IN THE FACE OF HIM!

AH, MERRY, STANDING FOR CAP'N AGAIN? YOU'RE A PUSHING LAD, TO BE SURE.

MATES, THERE'S TWO OF THEM ALONE THERE-- THE OLD CRIPPLED THAT BLUNDERED US AND A CUB I MEAN TO HAVE THE HEART OF.

NOW, MATES!

AHH!

URK!

BLAM BLAM

BLAM

GEORGE, I RECKON I SETTLED YOU.

FORWARD!

WE MUST HEAD 'EM OFF THE BOATS!

WE COULD SEE THEM RUNNING RIGHT FOR MIZZENMAST HILL AND REALIZED WE WERE ALREADY BETWEEN THEM AND THE BOATS, SO NOTHING WAS HURRYING US.

THANK YE KINDLY, DOCTOR.

YOU CAME IN THE NICK OF TIME. AND SO IT'S YOU, BEN GUNN!

AND HOW DO, MR. SILVER? PRETTY WELL, I THANK YE, SAYS YOU.

BEN, BEN, TO THINK AS YOU'VE DONE ME!

THE DOCTOR SENT BACK GRAY FOR ONE OF THE PICKAXES DESERTED BY THE MUTINEERS, WHILE WE PROCEEDED LEISURELY DOWNHILL.

HE TOLD US A STORY IN WHICH BEN GUNN WAS THE HERO FROM BEGINNING TO END.

IT WAS HE THAT HAD RIFLED THE SKELETON, HAD FOUND THE TREASURE, HAD DUG IT UP AND CARRIED IT TO A CAVE WHERE HE HAD SLEPT SINCE.

IT WAS AFTER WORMING THIS SECRET FROM HIM THAT THE DOCTOR HAD DECIDED TO GIVE THE CHART TO SILVER AND ABANDONED THE BLOCKHOUSE TO MOVE INTO THE HILLS WHERE THEY WOULD BE CLEAR OF MALARIA AND KEEP GUARD UPON THE MONEY.

THAT MORNING, KNOWING WHAT AWAITED THE MUTI-NEERS, HE GONE IN SEARCH OF GRAY AND GUNN AND HAD DIS-PATCHED THE LATTER ON BEFORE TO DO HIS BEST IN WORKING UPON THE SUPERSTITIONS OF HIS FORMER SHIPMATES.

AH, IT WAS FORTUNATE FOR ME THAT I HAD HAWKINS HERE. YOU WOULD HAVE LET OLD JOHN BE CUT TO BITS AND NEVER GIVEN IT A THOUGHT!

NOT A THOUGHT.

WE ALL GOT ABOARD A GIG WHILE THE DOCTOR DEMOLISHED THE OTHER WITH THE PICKAX.

SILVER, THOUGH EXHAUSTED, WAS SET TO AN OAR AND WE SKIMMED SWIFTLY OVER A SMOOTH SEA, DOUBLED THE SOUTHEAST CORNER OF THE ISLAND, ROUND WHICH, FOUR DAYS AGO, WE HAD TOWED THE *HISPANIOLA*.

AS WE PASSED THE TWO-POINTED HILL, WE SALUTED THE SQUIRE, WHO WAS STANDING GUARD AT THE BLACK MOUTH OF BEN GUNN'S CAVE.

THREE MILES FARTHER, JUST INSIDE THE MOUTH OF NORTH INLET, WHAT SHOULD WE MEET BUT THE *HISPANIOLA*.

THE LAST FLOOD HAVING LIFTED HER, SHE WAS CRUISING BY HERSELF.

HAD THERE BEEN MUCH WIND OR A STRONG TIDE CURRENT, WE SHOULD NEVER HAVE FOUND HER MORE.

WE ALL PULLED ROUND AGAIN TO RUM COVE, THE NEAREST POINT FOR BEN GUNN'S CAVE, AND IT WAS DECIDED GRAY WAS TO PASS THE NIGHT ON GUARD ABOARD THE SHIP.

THE SQUIRE MET US AT THE ENTRANCE OF THE CAVE. TO ME HE WAS CORDIAL AND KIND.

SQUIRE--

JOHN SILVER, YOU ARE A VILLAIN AND IMPOSTOR. I AM TOLD I AM NOT TO PROSECUTE YOU, BUT THE DEAD MEN, SIR, HANG AROUND YOUR NECK LIKE MILLSTONES.

THANK YOU KINDLY, SIR.

I DARE YOU TO THANK ME!

AND THEREUPON WE ALL ENTERED THE CAVE.

WHAT BLOOD AND SORROW, WHAT GOOD SHIPS SCUTTLED ON THE DEEP, WHAT SHAME AND LIES AND CRUELTY?

HOW MANY HAD IT COST?

NO MAN ALIVE COULD TELL.

COME IN, JIM. YOU'RE A GOOD BOY IN YOUR LINE, BUT TOO UNDISCIPLINED FOR MY LIKING.

SILVER, WHAT BRINGS YOU HERE?

COME BACK TO MY DOOTY, SIR.

AH!

WHAT A SUPPER I HAD OF IT THAT NIGHT WITH ALL MY FRIENDS!

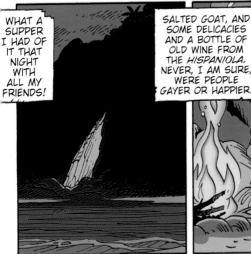

SALTED GOAT, AND SOME DELICACIES AND A BOTTLE OF OLD WINE FROM THE *HISPANIOLA*. NEVER, I AM SURE, WERE PEOPLE GAYER OR HAPPIER.

SILVER EVEN JOINED QUIETLY IN OUR LAUGHTER, THE SAME BLAND, POLITE, OBSEQUIOUS SEAMAN OF THE VOYAGE OUT.

THE NEXT MORNING WE FELL EARLY TO WORK FOR THE TRANSPORTATION OF THIS GREAT MASS OF GOLD WAS A CONSIDERABLE TASK.

THE THREE FELLOWS STILL ABROAD DID NOT GREATLY TROUBLE US; A SINGLE SENTRY ON THE SHOULDER OF THE HILL WAS SUFFICIENT.

GRAY AND BEN GUNN CAME AND WENT WITH THE BOAT, WHILE THE REST PILED TREASURE ON THE BEACH.

AS I WAS NOT MUCH USE AT CARRYING, I KEPT BUSY IN THE CAVE, PACKING THE MINTED MONEY INTO BREAD BAGS.

DOUBLOONS AND DOUBLE GUINEAS, THE PICTURES OF THE KINGS OF EUROPE, STRANGE ORIENTAL PIECES, ROUND AND SQUARE PIECES, AND THEN SOME.

NEARLY EVERY VARIETY OF MONEY FOUND A PLACE THERE.

DAY AFTER DAY THIS WORK WENT ON, AND ALL THIS TIME WE HEARD NOTHING OF THE MUTINEERS.

AT LAST, ONE EVENING, DURING A STROLL, THE WIND BROUGHT US A NOISE BETWEEN SHRIEKING AND SINGING.

RAHAAAA A YO-HO-HO

HEAVEN FORGIVE THEM.

MY FEELINGS MAY SURPRISE YOU, MASTER SILVER, BUT IF I WERE SURE THEY WERE RAVING FROM FEVER AND NOT DRUNKENNESS, I SHOULD IMMEDIATELY TAKE THEM THE ASSISTANCE OF MY SKILL.

ASK YOUR PARDON, SIR, YOU WOULD BE VERY WRONG. BUT THESE MEN DOWN THERE, THEY COULDN'T KEEP THEIR WORD AND THEY COULDN'T BELIEVE AS YOU COULD.

NO, YOU'RE THE MAN TO KEEP YOUR WORD, WE KNOW THAT.

A COUNCIL WAS HELD, AND IT WAS DECIDED THAT WE MUST DESERT THEM ON THE ISLAND, TO THE HUGE GLEE OF BEN GUNN.

WE LEFT A GOOD STOCK OF POWDER AND SHOT, OF THE SALTED GOAT, A FEW MEDICINES, AND SOME OTHER NECESSARIES, TOOLS, AND TOBACCO.

ONE FINE MORNING, WE WEIGHED ANCHOR AND STOOD OUT OF NORTH INLET.

AND WHEN LYING NEAR THE SOUTHERN POINT, WE SAW ALL THREE OF THEM KNEELING TOGETHER ON A SPIT OF SAND, WITH THEIR ARMS RAISED IN SUPPLICATION.

IT WENT TO ALL OUR HEARTS, BUT WE COULD NOT RISK ANOTHER MUTINY, AND IT WOULD HAVE BEEN CONDEMNING THEM TO THE GIBBET TO TAKE THEM HOME WITH US.

THE DOCTOR TOLD THEM WHERE WE HAD LEFT THEM THE STORES, BUT THEY CONTINUED TO APPEAL TO US TO NOT LEAVE THEM TO DIE IN SUCH A PLACE.

AT LAST, SEEING THE SHIP STILL BORE ON HER COURSE--

GRR!!

DLAM

T'CHAK

BEFORE NOON, TO MY INEXPRESSIBLE JOY, THE HIGHEST ROCK OF THE ISLE HAD SUNK INTO THE BLUE ROUND OF SEA.

WE WERE SO SHORT OF MEN THAT EVERYONE ON BOARD HAD TO WORK UNDER THE ORDERS OF THE CAPTAIN LYING ON A MATTRESS.

WE LAID COURSE FOR THE NEAREST PORT IN ORDER TO RECRUIT FRESH HANDS FOR THE VOYAGE HOME.

IT WAS JUST AT SUNDOWN WHEN WE CAST ANCHOR IN A LANDLOCKED GULF AND WERE IMMEDIATELY SURROUNDED BY SHORE BOATS FULL OF NEGROES AND MEXICAN INDIANS, SELLING FRUITS AND VEGETABLES.

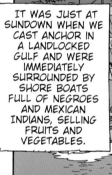

THEIR FACES, THE TASTE OF THE FRUITS, AND THE LIGHTS OF THE TOWN MADE A MOST CHARMING CONTRAST TO OUR DARK AND BLOODY SOJOURN ON THE ISLAND.

I ACCOMPANIED THE DOCTOR AND THE SQUIRE ASHORE WHERE WE PASSED THE EVENING, INDEED THE NIGHT, AFTER HAVING MET AN ENGLISH CAPTAIN.

WHEN DAWN SAW US COME ALONGSIDE THE SHIP, GUNN EXPLAINED TO US, WITH WONDERFUL CONTORTIONS THAT--

SILVER WAS GONE.

THE MAROON HAD CONNIVED AT HIS ESCAPE IN A SHORE BOAT SOME HOURS AGO.

HE ASSURED US HE HAD ONLY DONE SO TO PRESERVE OUR LIVES.

SO LONG AS THAT MAN WITH THE ONE LEG HAD STAYED ABOARD, WE WERE ALL OF US IN DANGER!

THE SEA COOK HAD NOT GONE EMPTY-HANDED. HE HAD CUT THROUGH A BULKHEAD AND REMOVED A SACK OF COINS.

I THINK WE WERE ALL PLEASED TO BE SO CHEAPLY QUIT OF HIM.

FINALLY, WE GOT A FEW HANDS ON BOARD, MADE A GOOD CRUISE HOME, AND THE *HISPANIOLA* REACHED BRISTOL JUST AS MR. BLANDLY WAS BEGINNING TO THINK OF FITTING OUT HER CONSORT.

FIVE MEN ONLY OF THOSE WHO HAD SAILED RETURNED WITH HER.

DRINK AND THE DEVIL HAD DONE FOR THE REST.

WE ALL SHARED THE TREASURE AND USED IT ACCORDING TO OUR NATURES.

CAPTAIN SMOLLETT IS NOW RETIRED FROM THE SEA.

GRAY IS MARRIED, THE FATHER OF A FAMILY, AND MATE OF A SHIP.

BEN GUNN SPENT OR LOST THE THOUSAND POUNDS HE HAD GOTTEN IN EXACTLY NINETEEN DAYS.

OF SILVER WE HEARD NO MORE AND I DARESAY HE STILL LIVES SOMEWHERE IN COMFORT WITH HIS WOMAN.

THE BAR SILVER AND THE ARMS STILL LIE WHERE FLINT BURIED THEM.

AND CERTAINLY THEY SHALL LIE THERE FOR ME, FOR NOTHING IN THE WORLD WOULD I RETURN TO THAT ACCURSED ISLAND.

THE WORST DREAMS THAT EVER I HAVE ARE WHEN I START UPRIGHT IN BED WITH THE SHARP VOICE OF CAPTAIN FLINT STILL RINGING:

THE END

WATCH OUT FOR PAPERCUT

Welcome to the fifth volume of the all-new CLASSICS ILLUSTRATED DELUXE series. I'm your humble editor, Jim Salicrup, here to tell you a little bit about Papercutz, the graphic novel publisher that's proud to present these beautiful adaptations of "Stories by the World's Greatest Authors."

We hope you enjoyed David Chauvel, Fred Simon, and Jean-Luc Simon's comics adaptation of Robert Louis Stevenson's Treasure Island. Unlike the earlier incarnations of CLASSICS ILLUSTRATED in which creators were limited to adapting classic novels in a mere 48 pages or so, you can see what a difference almost a hundred more pages makes. But even so, our adaptors still must cut and trim dialogue to fit the entire story, but we believe they've done it so skillfully, so respectfully, that fans of the original will be pleased.

And speaking of Robert Louis Stevenson fans, if you're one, you'll also want to check out John K. Synder III's adaptation of Dr. Jekyll & Mr. Hyde in the seventh volume of our companion series CLASSICS ILLUSTRATED. It's a highly stylized work, with dynamic layouts, and vibrant colors, that offer an interesting, yet still totally faithful adaptation.

And speaking of faithful adaptations, look what Derek Parker Royal wrote in MARK TWAIN ANNUAL about CLASSICS ILLUSTRATED DELUXE #4 "The Adventures of Tom Sawyer"…

> Morvan, Voulyze, and Le Fevebvre's adaptation of *Tom Sawyer* is a deluxe title that is much more faithful to Twain's novel than Michael Ploog's1990 version. The latter, which was limited to 48 pages …, eliminated or truncated a number of episodes from Twain's original story, e.g., the Sunday school events in chapters 4 and 5, Aunt Polly's homeopathic treatment of Tom in chapter 12, Becky tearing Mr. Dobbins's anatomy book in chapter 20, and the examination day performances in chapter 21. While manyof these scenes may seem tangential to many readers—although Twain's *Tom Sawyer* is structured episodically, complicating any questions of "secondary" action—the Papercutz edition retains them and, in this way, is "truer" than
> any of the earlier *Classics Illustrated* renditions. …the creators of the Papercutz volume employ the full range of manga flourish, including bold motion lines, skewed perspectives, and text-free sequencing that accentuates the action. This becomes a significant feature of the text, given fact that most of *Tom Sawyer* is plot-driven and relies heavily on episodic movement.

We should point out that we also greatly admire Mike Ploog's adaptation of Tom Sawyer, and ask for your advice – should we also bring it back into print in CLASSICS ILLUSTRSATED or not? Let us know. Also, let us know what you think of this volume and any other Papercutz edition of CLASSICS ILLUS-TRATED. Send feedback to us at salicrup@papercutz.com, or post you comments on the Papercutz Bog at www.papercutz.com, or write to us at: CLASSICS ILLUSTRATED, c/o Papercutz, 40 Exchange Place, Ste. 1308, New York, NY 10005.

Thanks,

ROBERT LOUIS STEVENSON

Robert Louis Stevenson (1850 –1894), born into a large Scottish family of engineers, is a child of fragile health whose schooling is haphazard. Not particularly interested in studying, he pursues a career as a writer. Bending to family tradition, however, he studies engineering at the university while simultaneously leading a dissolute life. In 1871, he chooses to redirect himself towards legal studies. Although he passes the bar exam, he never will practice law. In 1878, he publishes his first work, *An Inland Voyage*, in which he tells of travels in France and Belgium.

His first great success, *Treasure Island*, appears in 1883. He next publishes the extraordinary novella *The Strange Case of Dr. Jekyll and Mr. Hyde* (1886), which immediately finds immense success. In 1890, he settles permanently in Samoa in Oceania, in order to treat his tuberculosis. He devotes himself particularly to life on the island and takes a position against German imperialism, without, however, neglecting his literary career. Until his death, he writes many other novels, including *The Wrong Box, The Wrecker*, and also *The Ebb-Tide*.

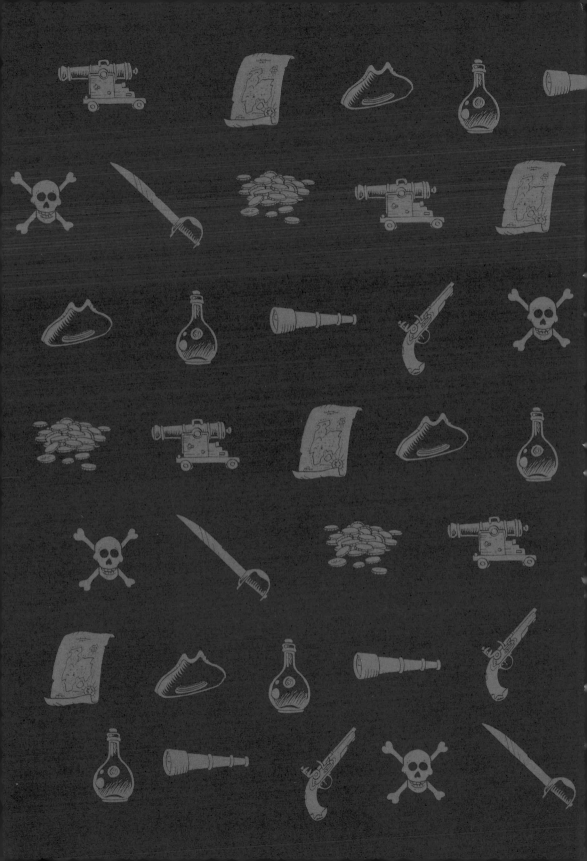